Cowpats and Brickbats

Tales from the Waikato

Cowpats and Brickbats
Tales from the Waikato

David Henshaw & Graham McBride

David Bateman

Also by David Henshaw, with John Dawson, *Whitebait & Wetlands: Tales of the West Coast* (Bateman, 1998).

Disclaimer: This is a collection of tales that the authors have heard during their many years living in the Waikato. Some stories are factual and were witnessed by, or recounted first-hand to, the authors. Others probably had their origins in a real incident, but over time and through many re-tellings have been embellished to create a good story. And quite a few cannot be verified at all and have become part of the folklore of farming and the Waikato, and so are included on that basis. In many cases, names and locations have been changed. The few genuine names are either historical figures or have been used with the permission of the person or their family. Any other name used that belongs to a person, living or dead, is entirely coincidental and no offence is intended.

Text © David Henshaw and Graham McBride, 2010
Illustrations © David Henshaw, 2010
Typographical design © David Bateman Ltd, 2010

First published in 2010 by David Bateman Ltd,
30 Tarndale Grove, Albany, Auckland, New Zealand

ISBN 978-1-86953-713-5

David Henshaw's colour cartoons reproduced with permission from *Jock's Country Life* (Allen Calendars, 2007). Also thanks to the family of Bill Richards, author of *Off the Sheep's Back* (Benton-Guy, 1991) and *A Pioneer's Life* (Benton-Guy, 1989); Mary Hurst, *Footprints in History*, No. 19, February 1998; C. W. Vennell & Susan Williams, *Raglan County Hills and Sea. A Centennial History 1876–1976* (Wilson & Horton, 1976).
Book design: WYSIWYG Design
Printed in China through Everbest Printing Co.

Contents

Mt Pirongia and the hills of Paterangi.

DAVID HENSHAW.

A Note from the Authors

Hard times and hard lives generate hard-case characters, and with them go a host of yarns. Tucked away beneath the current veneer of the Waikato's green pastures and four-wheelers there is a pioneering background of years of hard labour, drudgery, improvisation and doing without. Those are our unsung heroes.

A generation or two down the track we all benefit from the sheer bloody-minded persistence of those pioneer families who turned peat swamps and untrackable hills into the multimillion-dollar dairy and sheep farms that now dominate the whole area.

There is an old saying that if you didn't laugh you'd just sit down and cry. We have no doubt that the latter happened fairly often – but there *was* a lot of laughter. Those pioneers and the more recent Waikato residents have left behind a fair bunch of stories. Some of these yarns are based on those stories. Some are bull dust. Others lurk somewhere in between. And if they are not exactly and precisely true … they are the stuff that time and the re-telling may have 'embellished' and made into legends.

Along the way of creating these stories and this book there are people who we wish to acknowledge — the people who have wittingly and in some cases unwittingly contributed to components of this volume. In particular, we thank Wally Richards (of the 'Farming Family' family), Herb Smith, Doug Hartstone, Bill Clow, Steve Lowry, Don McNaughton, Graeme Cairns, Pete Hayes, Alan Kempthorne, Felix and Pete Davy, David Peart, Murray Powell and a heap of others who requested to remain anonymous for a number of rather legitimate and intriguing reasons.

This book is a tribute to those who persisted, made mischief and laughed and, at the end of the day, made it all happen in the Waikato.

David Henshaw & Graham McBride, 2010

1 The *Real* Farming Family of the Waikato

At the north end of Victoria Street, Hamilton, stands an evocative statue that celebrates the pioneer spirit of the Waikato – mum, dad, the two kids, the cow and the ewe, and the quintessential stock dog. The 'Farming Family' sculpture immortalises in bronze the 'unsung heroes of the ordinary pioneering families and the unsung heroes of the past 150 years,' according to donor Sir Robert Jones.

What is disconcerting is that extensive polling reveals that 99% of Waikato doesn't know the many stories behind the statues: the raison d'être for the sculpture; the unintentional slighting of the inspiration behind the statues; and the taking of the piss at the grand unveiling by the McGillicuddy Serious Party. Three events – all interconnected and all contributing to the mana of Waikato's 'Farming Family'.

The raison d'être

In the 1980s Sir Robert Jones had substantial assets in the city of Hamilton. He had a great interest in the city's success and was looking for a way of 'giving back' to the community. Sir Robert's reading of the book *Off the Sheep's Back* – the tale of a family's hard graft and privation – by former Te Akau resident and Master Shearer Bill Richards was the inspiration for the largesse.

Thus the 'Farming Family' statue was commissioned

David Henshaw's 'Farming Family'

as a commemoration to all the unsung pioneer families in the Waikato who, despite great hardship, succeeded in laying the foundations for the huge agricultural industry that exists in the region today. The statue cost $200,000 in 1990 and was designed and made by Timaru sculptor Margriet Windhausen-van den Bergh.

The unveiling

On 9 November 1990 more than 500 people gathered at the north end of Victoria Street to celebrate the unveiling of the 'Farming Family' sculpture. Ulster Street was blocked off for the event and chairs were laid out for invited guests. It was a big deal!

The unveiling was undertaken by Sir Peter Elworthy – a prominent Canterbury farmer – other dignitaries including Sir Robert Jones, Mayor Margaret Evans, Environment Waikato and Hamilton City Councillor David Peart and Sir Michael Fowler. During Sir Robert's speech, he alluded to the inspiration behind the statue – while on a flight to England he read Bill Richards' evocative book about his family's battles of cutting and burning the Te Akau bush to create pastureland. Sir Bob alluded to the many hardships families endured in the pioneering days both in the Waikato and throughout New Zealand and wished to do something to perpetuate the memory and history as a tribute to a 'vanished' generation.

Ironically, immediately after the formalities David Peart asked Sir Robert, 'Would you like to meet the author?'

Sir Robert, and others who organised the function, had assumed that Bill Richards was long dead. Peart explained that he was chair of the Central Baptist Church and Bill Richards lived in one of their pensioner flats, and was very much alive. The celebratory parade started down Victoria Street, led by two Clydesdale horses and a wagon, with the three 'Sirs' and Mayor Evans in pride of place, followed by a line up of vintage cars.

Meanwhile, David Peart literally plucked Bill from his flat and caught up with the parade – belatedly installing him on the lead wagon with the dignitaries. In Bill Richards' memoirs he explains: 'I was having a quiet chat with a couple of friends when there was this frantic knocking on the door. I was told, "You are supposed to be at the unveiling. Bob Jones is very annoyed. Get ready." I responded, "I think you have come to the wrong house. I have never heard about an unveiling, nor do I know a Bob Jones, so what is all the fuss about."'

At the completion of the parade a civic luncheon was held at the Hamilton Museum where Sir Robert introduced Bill Richards and spoke at length about *Off the Sheep's Back*, and how it inspired the idea of a monument. He also expressed regret that Bill hadn't been present at the unveiling.

Peart explains: 'The outcome of that meant that the parade down Victoria Street was rather special for both

Bill and for Sir Bob.' After the unexpected excitement of the day, Bill penned a story 'Three Knights in One Day' to celebrate the 'Farming Family' statue and the subsequent excitement with all the Sirs.

Living monuments.

While the Sirs and other guests were preparing to unveil the statue, Graeme Cairns and actor Merophie Carr of the McGillicuddy Serious Party were about to add their perspective to the event. The McGillicuddys had been undertaking silent street theatre around New Zealand for some years and had several central acts in their repertoire including 'the Swamp Stomp' and a gumboot dancing group.

Dressed in 1950s farm clothing, and completely covered from tip to toe in gray swamp mud, these extroverts 'oozed' through the distinguished guests and into the 'Farming Family' cluster – complete with an empty beer crate, a length of No. 8 fencing wire and a length of alkathene water pipe. The mud-covered pair mimed their way through some agrarian moves – including putting the farming missus 'on a beer crate pedestal' and checking for leaks in the water pipe. Cairns described this as completely unscripted theatre which wasn't aimed at 'taking the piss' so much as 'adding to a historically significant event with our special kind of art to make people think.'

Despite the official sense of decorum required by such an outstanding civic occasion, Sir Peter described the mime group's allegory as 'fantastic' in his speech. Mayor Evans was highly amused and Councillor Peart thought it was 'the funniest thing he had ever seen.' However, McGillicuddy's Cairns thought Sir Robert 'appeared to be pretty grumpy about the whole thing' – possibly annoyed at the unexpected additions to the statue.

———— *** ————

The 'Farming Family' endures. A clique of city residents wants to relegate the 'Farming Family', as McGillicuddy succinctly states 'to the back of some obscure garden in the back of some park somewhere.' These statue-averse residents view the prominent family as a millstone around Hamilton's growth – they consider that on entering the city, visitors (Aucklanders in particular) see the statue as a signpost that it is perhaps still a provincial cow town. Even the original negotiations for the positioning of the statues by the Hamilton City Council 'caused a hang of a row' according to Councillor David Peart, with debate raging about finding the 'appropriate' place for the 'Farming Family'.

Sadly, few Hamiltonians are aware of the meaning behind the 'Farming Family' statue – the families that broke the rough land of scrub and forest, swamp and hills of the Waikato with axe and grubber, and who, like Bill Richards at Te Akau, survived by doing without; for example, routinely eating what was immediately available – kiwi, tui, kereru, weka and nikau palm.

Even in 2009, when I interviewed McGillicuddy's Cairns, he, like almost all Waikato'ites, was unaware that the 'Farming Family' was 'real' – unaware that the statue was inspired by Bill Richards' memories. In the years since the unveiling McGillicuddys have gone on to add the 'Farming Family' to their repertoire and indeed use it as a mainstay of their street mime and theatre.

This general lack of awareness within the Waikato and Hamilton communities possibly explains why some see the statue as a hindrance to the region's growth and want it banished to where the 'Farming Family' can no longer embarrass. However, the statue is a clear and unambiguous sign that Hamilton is a city with its own identity – and unmistakably brands us as a very big and dynamic agriculture service centre.

Hamilton – be proud of your pioneering heritage and our human monuments! Leave the 'Farming Family' in the front paddock.

2 The Barking Gecko

If you subscribe to Newton's law of physics that every action has an equal and opposite reaction, then you may understand the consequences of William eating a whole can of baked beans in one sitting. The scene is a mountain hut on Maungatautari, an ecological reserve in the central Waikato.

This particular day, three separate parties arrived at the hut and were preparing their grub for the evening. Present are seven people: Don, hiking solo, a mature local of scholarly bearing and a wonderful sense of humour; William and his two mates – all younger Kiwis; and three Yanks and a German who'd sort of teamed up on the hike. This latter group were on the obligatory 'big OE' and their common interest was a fascination with New Zealand's unique flora and fauna. They weren't just interested in birds, bugs and bogs; they were inhaling our whole ecosystem. 'Fritz' even had some reference books on ornithology and entomology, and the four of them could discuss whether their sighting of a harrier hawk at 700 metres was in fact a bald eagle or the Great Plains spotted vulture. Sorta nerdy really, but nice enough guys.

William had consumed a whole can of baked beans (all 434 of them) on an empty stomach and, to his considerable chagrin, every one of them was working their way through his digestive system – embarrassingly so. The manifestations of this weren't in the nature of common flatulence – they were of a very sharp, very loud and incredibly smelly nature. So much so, that William would discreetly disappear out of the hut periodically to unload, dead scared that the combined release of two beans together would have serious and unintended consequences.

As everybody cooked their meals in the communal kitchen and discussed the hike and the local wildlife, William would ooze outside and sprint around the hut leaving a trail of sonic claps. So, against the background of general meal preparation and buzz of conversation there was this occasional resonance of … well … 'barks' that emerged from the scrub surrounding the hut. Nothing was said, but the Kiwis were amused at William's efforts to be subtle about his sudden bouts of back pressure.

After dinner, everyone was spread out around the front door of the hut – some lounging in the doorway, some on the steps. William was perched on the extreme end of the bench, ready to cut a track. A few were smoking, all were admiring the Southern Cross stars, and, over the sound of the rushing stream below, a ruru – the morepork – called. Beautiful. In the background was an occasional but distinctive noise – brrrk – that seemed to emerge from different parts of the scrub.

During the after-dinner yarning Don had emerged as something of an authoritative father figure on New Zealand's nature so it was logical when Fritz asked, 'Vas is dat barking noise ve hear occasionally?' that Don would reply.

'Well,' says Don, straight-faced, 'that is our incredibly rare native barking gecko.' The visitors dived into their reference books and looked up geckos: *Hoplodactylus granulatus*, or forest gecko; *Hoplodactylus maculatus*, the common gecko, but no barking geckos.

So, naturally, the questions started and, naturally, Don was required to respond. The trouble was that the more he elaborated on the lifestyle of the native barking gecko, the more he had to shovel the bullshit.

'Oh, this is an incredibly rare species – it was first described by a Mr Wattie from Napier in the early '60s. It is almost ethereal in its presence, is incredibly difficult to sight and when it does manifest itself the finder generally considers it an unpleasant experience.'

'Awesome,' breathed one of the Yanks. 'A fantastically rare animal and we're here to witness it.

14

How do they breed?' he asked.

'Well, no one is quite sure of the process,' said Don, 'but what you can hear is thought to be the mating call.'

'Do ze females bark also?'

Don, ad-libbing like hell said, 'Yes they do, but their replies are believed to be more muted and subtle than the male of the species.'

Meanwhile, William was slinking off into the darkness every so often and doing his 'bark and bolt' bit. His two Kiwi mates had also bolted – off the veranda and into their bunkroom. Therein could be heard muffled shrieks as they tried to stifle their gut-busting mirth by chewing on the insides of their sleeping bags.

Don, straight-faced as ever, continued the detailed explanation on the fascinating sex life of the native barking gecko.

'The juvenile female of the species appears to be very active but somehow when they become "attached" to a male the libido inclination seems to decline rapidly.'

And so the evening continued.

Finally, the Kiwis all retired to bed, leaving Fritz and the Yanks on their hands and knees crawling around in the damp manuka with a candle trying to catch a barking gecko. Completely oblivious to the barely controlled mirth from the local contingent, and William's occasional absences, breakfast was a detailed reconstruction of the late-night hunt for the elusive beast.

Finally, the visitors set off for the next hut, determined to demonstrate their world-class authority on this unique critter to anyone and everyone. Don and his partners-in-crime, having established that the natural history 'experts' were out of earshot, lay on the floor and between side-splitting bellows and tears down their faces, undertook a post-mortem on the evening's entertainment. And where was William during all this?

Brrrk, number 338, brrrk, number 339, brrrk …

3 Never Say Never

The flash new vet arrived on Herb's farm at 'The 2 Whatas', as the locals call it (aka Whatawhata), complete with shiny overalls, pristine gummies and a university-inspired air of confidence. Plus a mint, straight-off-the-shelf Ford Laser with only 350 calamities on the clock. Vet Andy, the owner, was just so proud to be out in the *real* world saving the ill animals of the west of Hamilton and beyond.

So Andy arrives at Herb's for a cow with a crook foot and parks right in front of the raised cattle-loading race. Herb, coincidentally, has a badly bloated cow up the loading race – facing uphill trying to get it to belch up the methane gas that is going to kill it if it doesn't burp it up.

Andy queries what Herb is up to. He explains that he's done this for years – placing the near-death bovine in the uphill position allows the gas to be regurgitated and the animal gradually deflates.

'But won't she jump out of the loading race?' is the next question.

'Never,' says Herb. 'I've done this hundreds of times and the cows are that pleased to get some relief that once they get their heads up the ramp they don't move!'

'Well, I'll be darned,' says the new vet.

Ten minutes later, the other cow, with its sore foot attended to, is a lot happier and on its way back down the farm when 'crash' and 'smash' and even 'bash, bash, bash' reverberates around the yard. Herb and Andy sprint around the corner to see the bloated animal thrashing her way across the roof of the sadly sagging Laser. Never say never!

Maungatautari, looking across Rotomanuka.

Remember what it was y'said that offended' 'im so next time 'e shows'
up y'can use it again.

4 Big Goolies

Sam the trucker was taking a load of beef from two different farms in the central Waikato all the way to the freezing works in Hawke's Bay. He'd collected some big prime ox first, and loaded the front three pens in his Hino transporter. The final stop was at Roger the Dodger's farm to fill the last, or rearmost, pen on the truck.

Says Roger, 'You've got eleven hours of driving in front of you mate – nip over to the house cause Mum's cooked you a feed and you won't have to stop on the way then.' Somewhat reluctantly Sam is coerced into putting on the bib for a few minutes. The clincher was that Roger would load his own cattle in the back pen of the truck while Sam had the nose bag on.

Some eleven hours later, and in the dead of night, a tired Sam reaches the works and unloads the truck. Now he might be knackered but out of the dark Sam is amazed to see that the front pen's cattle have somehow undergone a bit of shrinking – similar colour but smaller animals. 'What the hell?'

And all the way back to the Waikato he's scratching his head and trying to find the angle.

Finally he has it sussed! While Mum was keeping him busy, Roger, the artful dodger, had got some of his own inferior beef with similar colours to those in the front pens, unloaded the whole truck, pen by pen, and substituted his smaller cattle, reloaded the truck and then put his 'own' now much-larger cattle on as planned. The poor chap who'd sent his prime ox to the works must have wondered why the hell his carcase yields and grading were so poor … and Roger had effectively ripped him off with no way of anyone proving it!

Now pulling off a trick like that takes some *big* goolies.

5 Of Mountain Men

There is a wonderful Mountain Radio Service throughout New Zealand which allows trampers and campers, hunters and the like to keep track of pending weather events, call in for emergency help or go 'off channel' for more social talk or business calls. For those often in remote back-country areas, Mountain Radios are a very important link to the outside world, and the evening 'sked', the daily call to receive the weather forecast and record locations and intentions, and the following 'channel chat' become important ways of relieving the isolation.

You can picture the scene … remote huts and isolated camp sites scattered around the central North Island, and therein living bewhiskered and socially deprived possum trappers, goat cullers, climbers, bush workers, such as DOC staff, and hermits – not to mention blokes avoiding domestic responsibilities and the odd asylum seeker.

Dallas is just such a chap; sitting in a lonely bush hut on Maungatautari. Dallas is also in lust, as is his girlfriend who is pining for his return from the bush and really *really really* missing him.

Knowing Dallas has a Mountain Radio, she decides to hire one for the evening to have a little 'phone sex' and relieve a bit of tension.

Seems like a good idea, but what she doesn't understand is that the Mountain Radio Service is a *public* communications system. Unlike a mobile phone, conversations are not so much one-to-one as one-to-many.

'Oooh … Flipper.' (There is a collective gasp of amazement in countless other camps and huts at the revelation of Dallas's secret nickname.) 'I miss you *sooo* much.'

Dallas responds with some trepidation, thinking he's never going to live this one down next time he shows up at the local. 'Ah, sweety this is not a secure channel. Over.'

Sweety, oblivious to Dallas's subtle warning, continues with her plan. 'Oooh, Flipper, that last night together was *soooo* much fun.' (At this stage, bush boys all over are wondering what the hang trick he did to be called 'Flipper'.)

Dallas cuts across her broadcast 'Ah, Sweety. Look it's not a good time to talk like THIS. Over.'

Sweety (still oblivious), 'I so want to see you again and

Bush hut.

HENSHAW.

do what we did that night again – and again.'

Dallas, desperately caught between 'keeping his end up' for Sweety (so to speak) and cringing at the thought of guys all over sitting absolutely riveted to the radio, cuts across before Sweety can say 'Over.' 'Look, I'll come out and see you as soon as I can I (pause, cringe) love you and I gotta go.'

And so the conversation develops, until in desperation Dallas cuts in: 'I'm needed, the rice is burning. I'll come and see you as soon as I can. OVER AND OUT.'

Sweety, blissfully unaware of Dallas's humiliation, is still only just warming to the phone sex, and is left feeling more than a little frustrated. She signs off with much emotion … 'I love you Flipper.'

You can just imagine bush boys sitting glassy-eyed around the fire, oblivious to the blow-flies on their tucker, fags dangling, beer untested, overcome by Sweety's urgent tones.

Uncharacteristically, there is total silence across the ether. No flippant remarks, no uninvited comments. Just electronic static. Until a deep baritone voice finally cuts in, 'I luv you too Flipper.'

6 Kia Ora Katoa

I pulled up beside a stolen car which had been dumped and set on fire on the side of our road. While I was checking it out a cop arrived and we swapped bull dust for a few minutes. Then, as arranged by the cop, a truck appeared to uplift the dead car. Driving the tow truck was a weight-enhanced Maori chap – who, elbow out the window, obviously had to hold the door onto his truck.

The cop says to me, 'Watch this – I'm going to greet him in Maori,' and says to the truckie, 'Kia ora Car Tower.'

The tow truck driver was decidedly not amused.

7 Into the Valley of Te Akau Stumbled the Fifteen

We played at Te Akau once. Actually the team went over there every year, but I only made it once. I was doing a season on a dairy farm near Ohaupo and all able-bodied blokes who were worth their salt and liked their beer, and were able to appreciate a nice pair of legs, were roped in to maintain the district's pride. Or at least try to.

It was a day trip. We were to meet the bus outside the pub at 10 o'clock. It was shut at that time of day, which we thought was thoroughly unsporting but it was probably just as well. It was the same at Waingaro.

There followed 38 miles of hill-country roads, narrow and winding. We had to wait for a couple of blokes to clear a tree which had fallen across the road overnight and, at one stage, the bus driver made us all get out and walk as he inched the old Bedford bus along what was left of the road where a culvert had dropped out. We all agreed that these were good signs … the ground would at least be soft.

I did feel a bit car sick. Or, in this case, bus sick. Some of the bright bastards seemed to think if they asked me enough times I would probably make myself crook but I made it with breakfast intact.

The trip took forever, and after reaching Dunhill corner and being told we were there, '… well, just about there,' and winding our way up the hill, we crested the ridge and there, laid out before us, was the Te Akau valley. It was quite a sight, and still a ways to go, but the sun was shining out by the coast and our spirits lifted.

Everyone was there to greet us; with beer, and lots of food made by the good ladies of the district – homemade sandwiches, cakes, scones and pikelets. Someone had a big grill and a charcoal fire going turning out steaks that were just a wee bit underdone on the inside and lightly burnt on the outside. The hospitality was nothing short of brilliant.

It seemed a grave imposition when the ref wandered around blowing his whistle saying, 'Right you blokes, get into y'gear, there's a game to play.'

We tried to negotiate quarter times rather than a half time out but they wouldn't wear it. And then we tossed for which end we'd play. They won and said 'uphill'.

There was just a hint of a suspicion that things were not quite going our way with this game, especially when I thought back a bit and could not recall any of their players with a bottle of beer in their hands.

'Into the valley of Te Akau stumbled the fifteen,' I thought as we bravely marched out with Ohaupo's pride on our shoulders.

Then it rained. The clouds had been building off to the southwest for a couple of hours and finally it got to us. And it pelted down. The sticky clay loam clung to our boots, making each foot twice its normal weight, and the relief of playing downhill disappeared the instant we realised that we had to play uphill in the second half – when we'd be pretty much buggered anyway.

There was some respite when a fight broke out. One of the forwards got a knee in the face, which he took exception to and so grabbed the offending leg, followed it up and started to beat the shit out of the owner. It was all a big mistake really because they were both our blokes and in the mud, and the stress, and the heat of the moment, they just got a bit confused. The ref, very solemnly, made them shake hands and the game resumed.

There was another break when the ball got an almighty punt and, with the sou-westerly behind it, wound up in the pine trees beside the ground. There wasn't a spare so it took awhile for an agile bloke to climb and shake and prod with a long stick to dislodge it.

For the record we lost. But who cared? It was a good game, in a wonderful place, and the hospitality … oh boy!

8 Chief Isaacs

The Waikato River is a kaitiaki (guardian) of the Tainui people and in the tribe's well-known proverb reference is made to the river's many chiefs and noble people of influence (represented by the taniwha):

Waikato taniwha rau
He piko, he tanawha
He piko he taniwha

Waikato of a hundred taniwha
At every bend a taniwha can be found.

In pre-European times, another important river was the Waipa, which joins the Waikato River at 'the meeting of the waters' (Ngaruawahia). The Waipa was a very important highway for Maori – and was possibly one of the most used rivers in Aotearoa. Food and goods were widely traded up and down the river by canoe, and war parties used the river for egress and entry into the heartland of Waikato Tainui and Maniapoto territory.

Families or communities associated with the Waipa lived in pa or kainga – small settlements with hapu or family links. These were numerous and primarily linked to this stately river and its aquatic bounty – especially the pa-tuna or eel-weirs, strategically placed at each tributary and stream to catch this important food source.

Dr Ferdinand von Hochstetter was a geologist and early European explorer who ventured into the Waipa basin via the river in 1859. He described the region thus: 'The beautiful, richly cultivated country about Rangiaowahia [Rangiaohia] and Otawhao [Te Awamutu] lay spread out before me like a map … and church steeples of these places were seen arising from among orchards and fields. I could hardly realise that I was here in the interior of New Zealand.'

As the colony expanded, Maori seized the commercial opportunity and villagers grew crops such as flax, wheat, tobacco and maize to supply trading ships and later exported food to the fledgling town of Auckland, or further afield to Sydney and even California.

Initial colonial settlement in the Waipa basin saw the continued use of the Waipa River via Maori canoe and the eventual introduction of paddle steamers such as the *Bluenose* and *Rangariri*, which plied their trade up as far as Pirongia.

Forests of rimu, kahikatea, matai and even some kauri

were cut down and rafts of native timber logs floated to sawmills.

Even as late as the Second World War, sacks of fertiliser still came upriver by barge. However, with the advent of roading about this time most communities literally turned their backs on the river. Like other river-based communities along the Waipa, the Moehaaki Pa (which translates as 'we sleep under the stars'), near Te Kowhai, was gradually abandoned during the 1950s.

Even up until the 1950s the whares in the village were pretty basic, with earth floors and no running water. Extensive communal gardens were maintained by tribal ohu, or working bees, with kumara and potato mainstay food sources.

In this period the inhabitants were led by Chief Isaacs, a stern but stately person who was man enough to take on not one but three wives. 'Senior' Mrs Isaacs was beyond child-bearing age, Mrs Isaacs ('Punarua' or second wife) turned out not to be able to have children and so 'Junior' Mrs Isaacs had became the clan standard–bearer so to speak.

For many years Chief Isaacs would undertake excursions to Ngaruawahia to collect 'Social Security' or 'the pension' and get groceries. This was a somewhat formal process with the Chief regally sitting up front driving the Model A Ford, while his wives and children were relegated to sitting on the deck. However, petrol rationing and lack of car parts during the Second World War interrupted these visits. This was a period when almost everything was governed by coupons – even staple items such as meat, clothing, tea, sugar and fuel. It was a time of great shortage and restrictions.

A rural family's allocation of petrol was only four gallons a month (about 18 litres) and thus the chief's travels were severely curtailed. Improvisation was called for. So Chief Isaacs, having removed the almost useless engine from his motorcar, would hook up a horse to the front of the Model A and 'drive' to town to collect his benefit and to shop.

The Chief's 'one-horsepower' car was by no means unusual during these times. Bill Richards in *A Pioneer's Life* tells of a Te Akau resident who, unable to procure tyres and tubes for his early Ford during the Second World War, 'stuffed the old tyres with grass and fern' and continued to drive. Steve Lowry, a former farmer in the Ongarue district, recalls a farmer who was unable to get tubes through the early 1940s also stuffing his tyres with grass. 'He had to pack the tyres twice on the seven-mile drive to Ongarue … It was hilarious – it looked like bullocks had walked along the road spitting out chewed cud or balls of wadded up grass from inside the tyres. Then Pat got sick of the "grass-ware" and wound rope around the rims. He could get into the local village three times before the rope wore out.'

Anyway, these Moehaaki horses, such as Chief Isaacs used in his gas-free vehicle, were notorious – the so-called 'Maori horses' that haunted the wider community with their uncontrolled foraging. The horses could somehow spot an open gate from three miles away, and appeared to be able to release secure gate hasps. The 'Maori horses' made absolutely no distinction between vegetable gardens, flower gardens or hay paddocks, daylight predations or nocturnal raids. Everyone loathed them with a passion – bar their owners. The horses' mere presence down a distant road would trigger outrage and fear.

When Wallace spotted one of these nags lurking around his farm's front gate he dispatched 11-year-old Leonard to 'Get rid of that #@%!! horse once and for all… and teach it a bloody good lesson!'

Well, Leonard took to the horse with youthful vengeance – chasing it on his bicycle and repeatedly clouting it on the arse with a long manuka waddy. By the time Leonard had got to the end of the road, he'd whittled the waddy down to a shaving brush. Three miles later, the foundering nag, with its sides heaving massively and still with its bum being thrashed, staggered up to one of the whares. The pint-sized Leonard yelled his dad's message (verbatim) at the elderly woman resident: 'Why don't you keep your #@%!! horse at home!' Whereupon the horse at last succumbed to its unusual exertions and dropped dead at her feet from a heart attack.

Terrified at this unexpected turn of events, and fearful of the consequences, young Leonard bolted – arriving back home in nearly the same state as the horse had arrived at its owner's property.

Up to and even after the Second World War these were still tough times and everybody helped each other out. Local farmer Sid Saulbery was no exception – that is until he lent Moehaaki's inhabitants his prized sickle-bar hay mower and Fergie tractor. Having lectured them at great length about looking after the valuable mower blades, he became highly excited when driving past he spotted the tractor and mower moving along the road verge on the back of a truck (also borrowed). They weren't mowing grass as one would expect – they were

trimming the tops of a thick barberry hedge. Now mower blades were never designed for timber cutting and this really 'gapped Sid's axe!' Who would ever think of that trick to trim a hedge?

——— *** ———

Today, nothing physical remains of Moehaaki village beyond a lone fruit tree and the scrub-covered hill that once was a vital lookout up and down the Waipa River. Cattle graze contentedly where once Maori horses looked longingly at the kumara gardens. The barberry hedge is gone and Sid is mowing meadows in the sky with his (gapped) prized sickle-bar. Yet, despite the physical changes, the spirit of Chief Isaacs and his people remain with the land.

9 No Bull!

Rural landowners are very fortunate in that they can get the most tender, tastiest meat in New Zealand simply by slaughtering a prime young animal right where it is grazing. The 'home kill' expert (quite a different connotation to the urban 'home kill' scenario) drives onto the property and shoots the nominated animal, butchers it on the spot,

removes the offal and returns the pre-frozen and packaged meat around a week later. A wonderful service with no stress and no mess.

In comparison it's a wonder supermarket meat isn't like shoe leather. All that stress – mustering the animal, trucking it to the 'freezing works', hosing it down to clean it, starved for 24 hours and dispatched in a noisy abattoir that reeks of blood and guts.

The home kill recipient can become a bit complacent about high quality meat — but sometimes it can go horribly wrong. This yarn is about the case of mistaken identity and a freezer full of really tough meat. And that takes one hell of a lot of eating!

Wal, the on-the-farm home-kill expert from Koromatua way, received a call from Jimmy, a gumboot-dancer from just outside of Paterangi, to get a freezer beef processed. Wal told him he'd be there Tuesday week and asked where the animal would be. Jimmy thought for a mo' and said, 'It'll be on its own in the little paddock right beside the cow yard.'

The following Tuesday, about breakfast time, Wal turns up as planned and, finding nobody about, he slaughters the only beast to be seen – exactly as instructed.

A few mouthfuls into his bacon and eggs, Jimmy hears a distant shot and idly speculates to Mum about what silly sod would be using a large calibre rifle at this hour of the day. Half-way through his second cup of coffee a nasty thought flits through his mind that he is somehow connected to that rifle shot. Then, suddenly the idle speculative thoughts coalesce into panic – toast flying every which way, Jimmy is out the door slicker 'n cat shit on a linoleum floor.

Half-way through skinning the dead animal, Wal hears the sound of a distant farm bike screaming like a turpentined cat but thinks nothing further of it. He does, however, wonder why anyone would want to eat a humungous, dirty, ugly, old Hereford bull.

Turns out it was the first day of mating for the dairy herd and Jimmy had forgotten all about Wal turning up as arranged. Anyone for some rather large, very expensive and very tough mountain oysters?

10 **Russ**

Russ is a 'live-line' artist, one of those brave guys who go up power poles to sort out faults on power lines with a zillion volts still running through them. Such people are precise – they have to be, one mistake and they're toast. So what happened to Russ's rectum was a surprise to the two people privileged enough to hear the secret. One of them told me, and I feel duty-bound to reveal the story – but just this once.

Through an excessive diet of meat pies and copious amounts of warm beer, Russ's digestive system rebelled and he developed a very nasty case of piles (I cannot confirm this other than by hearsay). Now, I am assured bleeding piles are a particularly nasty torment and require extremely tender ministrations. Russ was prescribed an 'undie insert' – sort of like a large panty shield – and given instructions on how to apply the self-sticking, pain relief support. Well, despite 'precision' being his middle name, Russ applied the self-sticking support inside out. The screams of pain were heard all over the Waikato as the 'sticky stuff' was ripped from the tender parts… would you trust this guy to rewire your house?

Russ was also a fishing fanatic. When offered work as a temporary 'sparky' at the Karapiro Power Station, he figured things would be pretty dull until at smoko one of the Maori 'yardies' mentioned freshwater fishing to his mates. As all fishos seem to be able to do, Russ zeroed in on the conversation (my wife maintains there is some secret societal handshake or insignia tattooed on the foreheads of these creatures that transcends religion, race or creed) and learnt that a fish was 'on the books' after work that day. Showing the secret sign was enough to get Russ invited to the event – even though he had misgivings about the quantity and species of freshwater fish of the mighty Waikato River.

'Eh, how do I find you guys?'

'S'easy – just drive down Maungatautari Road till ya see the boys.'

'Right, I'll bring my gear.'

'Na bro, just turn up. We've got all the kit.'

So Russ arrives at a gathering of vehicles parked beside a 110,000 kilovolt power transformer and – what the hell! – there's a guy up the side of the trannie (not the Auckland variety!) with rubber gloves and a bloody great pair of electrical connectors. Leading out to the riverbank is a heavy insulated cable and a chap holding a really long pole with two bare wires exposed on the end.

To Russ's complete astonishment the guy up the transformer yells, 'Are you ready fullas?' to the waiting mob on the bank, and having received the necessary assurances, he clips the connectors to the super-hot side of the trannie. Half of Cambridge's lights must have dimmed as the now-smoking pole was dipped in the water and within seconds hundreds of stunned fish had surfaced in the river. With another yell the power was disconnected and everybody dived into the water to grab the fish.

Russ was looking at the biggest catch of fish he had ever seen, with not a hook in sight. Being a safety-conscious sort of chap he couldn't help but speculate on how the trick had been learnt and what would happen if the order of the process were mucked up. Who says fishermen aren't innovative!

11 Midnight Special

The celebration of Paul and Michelle's engagement was a fine time to bring together two large families, and set the scene for the pending marriage. Paul – a rambunctious lad – was dressed in his good duds and desperately trying to lay off the booze to ensure he put his best foot forward, so to speak.

So, out-laws and in-laws and friends are trying to mix and be sociable and check out the other team – sort of like dogs sniffing each other at a sheep dog trial. Well into the evening, one of the 'out-laws', Bunter, was in a group discussing the merits of various motorbikes. The current fad was for a fancy and very expensive set of wheels – the Yamaha 750cc 'Midnight Special' – and eventually the talk got around to the price of the beast.

'Hey Paul,' yells Bunter across a couple of mobs of people, 'How much for a Midnight Special?'

At exactly the moment he lobs his question, one of those funny silences opens up in the whole room – and everyone tunes into Paul's answer.

The son-in-law to-be, momentarily distracted from trying to impress the mother-in-law to-be, without thinking shoots back, 'Sixty bucks.'

Shame!

12 When Men Were Men

Felix and Ron Davy fenced for Ed Buckley in the King Country on and off for about 28 years. One of the first jobs the father-and-son team did for Ed was constructing a road fence over undulating land at 'Rangitoto'. In preparation, Ed had laid out a truck-load of strainers, angles, fence posts and battens along the newly bulldozed line.

Everything was hand dug and rammed at that time, but Felix and Ron were pretty efficient, and so they asked Ed to lay out another line for when they had finished the road fence.

'Don't you worry … these will last you quite a while,' was the reply.

So Ron and Felix decided to show Ed just how good they were. They set out 43 chains (about 900 metres) of wire and aimed to dig and ram in 200 posts on the first day. But, what with putting in angle posts, tie-downs and guide wires, they *only* managed 148 posts. In just two and a half days, Felix and Ron completed the whole fence, including stapling on 1150 battens. That's over 8000 staples.

In two weeks less than Ed had calculated, they used up all the fencing materials he had in stock. With nothing more they could do, Felix rang Ed to tell him they had to move on to another contract to give Ed time to truck in more materials.

Felix and Ron also worked for Bruce Galbraith, who was breaking in some new country that had no fences. Every year, on this one block alone, Felix and Ron would build between 7 and 15 kilometres of new fence. They also made and swung 280 wooden gates and used around 27,000 fence battens. One other year they built six sets of sheep yards, three sets of cattle yards (putting in 45 cattle yard strainers in one day) and erected about 60 kilometres of new fencing!

That is serious hard work!

When it comes ter strainin' up an old fence . . . yer gotta admit . . . e's quick!

13 The Great Waipa Flood of '58

Somewhere around 1842 an early explorer described the Waipa River thus:

'Nothing can exceed the quiet beauty of the banks of the Waipa. The hills rise gradually from the river side to a moderate elevation, clothed with magnificent forest, its luxuriance amply attesting the richness of the soil, and appearing as if nature intended them in future times as the residence of the aristocracy of New Zealand.'

Much of that explorer's prophetic statement came to pass. However, the plains and banks of the Waikato and Waipa Rivers and their environs have been a flood-prone part of the region since mankind set out to convert the largely undeveloped lands of the area into farmland.

The Waipa is still a 'wild river' – it is not controlled directly by any man-made structures.

The flood of 1958 hit the catchment of the Waipa very badly and the destruction of roads, crops, houses and property was the result. Livestock were swept away and milk collection was suspended in some areas.

Even today, flood levels are benchmarked against the '58.

The floods of 1998 and 2004, which did significant damage to urban property in Otorohanga and Huntly respectively, were mere pups in comparison – being almost two metres lower than the '58 at Whatawhata Bridge.

C. W. Vennell, in the book he co-wrote with Susan Williams, Raglan County Hills and Sea. A Centennial History 1876–1976, *described the January 1907 Waipa flood at Ngaruawahia as being '23 inches higher than the previous highest flood of 1875' and lapping the bottom of the then new rail bridge. He also mentioned that farmers were forced to dry feed livestock for many months as they tried to recover from the flood.*

Records show that Hamilton received over 11 inches of rain in seven days during this time, and another reference by Mary Hurst in Footprints of History *puts the 1907 flood level above Alexandra (Pirongia) at a massive '80 feet above normal summer river height' – somewhere above the height of the current high-level bridge between Te Rore and Te Pahu.*

The 'workings' of the Waipa River usually means that this river peaks before the Waikato River catchment floodwaters reach the confluence of the two rivers, thus avoiding the worst of any flooding. However, the pattern

Since you're insured would y'like to back up an' have another go at that old strainer y'missed on the way through!

Jackson Homestead, Karioi.

David Henshaw

of rain in February 1958 was markedly different in that the Waikato catchment received the bulk of its rain before the Waipa area got soaked. Rising flood water was spilt through the hydro dams on the Waikato with the result that both rivers peaked at the same time and the consequences of the Waipa stalling were devastating.

———— *** ————

Fred and Myrtle lived at Otorohanga, which was transformed in February 1958 from a quite rural service town into a Venice look-alike. Much of the town was affected, with two-thirds of its area under more than six feet of flood water, and row boats were used to rescue stranded people. Estimations were that about 1000 of the 1600 residents were billeted by more fortunate neighbours until the effects of the flood diminished.

However, there was an occasional upside to the '58 flood. Fred worked at the supermarket and one of his cleanup tasks was to remove all flood-affected foodstuffs from the shelves and take them to the dump.

Among the assortment of rotting and dirty vegetables and meats was a large quantity of canned foods – minus their labels, which had soaked off in the floodwaters.

Fred 'diverted' a large assortment of de-labelled cans from the dump to his garage, cunningly cached for later consumption. Over time, experience taught Fred's

family that selecting a can at random from the stack was fraught with risk. For many years 'Lucky Dip' was the ongoing entertainment for friends, rellies and family. Everyone sat up at the table with their pudding plates, knives and spoons and a food tin was selected from the heap. Anyone for ice cream and peas? How about Tip Top and baked beans? This became very much a family tradition and inevitably much hilarity resulted when the contents were revealed.

Food problems that required creative thinking also occurred further down the Waipa River. At one now-defunct village, granny had died and the cemetery was under water.

Coincidentally, the appliance company that had recently sold the family a new deep freezer had lost patience with the lack of repayments. Their agent was sent out to repossess the whiteware, and expecting the usual '23 reasons' and excuses why he should leave the item alone, was very pleased to be told 'it's out in the orchard in that shed – help yourself.'

Heading for the freezer with some relief he opened the lid to check the interior and very nearly had a heart attack. The flash new deep freeze had been requisitioned to keep Gran on ice till the waters receded and she could be buried. Needless to say, the freezer stayed put!

At Karakariki, the consequences of the '58 flood were more tragic. George Thomson was a big man who liked to be left alone. He lived up the tributary of the Timaru Stream, well up in the bush in a rough nikau whare. Being a committed recluse, George had made arrangements for his social security payments to be cashed in for food (and grog) by the storekeeper at Whatawhata.

Karakariki farmer Frank Duck would collect George's supplies and take them into him on horseback. This arrangement endured for a number of years and relied on the goodwill of Frank to purchase and deliver the life-sustaining (liquid) staples. However, the '58 flood blocked off vast areas of land, including all the Karakariki river-flats and the base of the Timaru Stream. When the floodwaters finally receded, Frank and another local, Charlie Bell, took the way-overdue supplies by horseback up to the whare and there they were greeted by a very belligerent and agitated George.

Blaming Frank for not delivering his food and booze, he yelled, 'I've had enough of this,' and promptly shot Frank in the chest with a .22 calibre rifle.

Frank and Charlie scarpered out of the Timaru on their horses and headed for Waikato Hospital, where minor surgery successfully fixed Frank's wound – although when he eventually died from old age he was buried with the bullet still in him. The police were called and, not knowing the area, requested the local farmer's guidance. 'That'll be the bloody day,' said Eric Sager – reflecting local feeling entirely.

Mounted constables were sent in to deal with George. And they did – George, with a severe bullet wound, came back out to civilization draped over a horse's saddle and he, too, was immediately hospitalised. There are different versions of how Thomson got his injury – no one is clear as to whether it was self-inflicted or a result of police intervention, but George died in hospital.

14 G'arn You Bastards

Te Pahu Ned had a clapped-out old totara fence in front of his house which was on his 'get round to it list'. The farm's mob of massive jet-black Angus bulls lived in the front paddock for a large portion of the calendar when they were banned from the ladies mobs. Boredom and frustration meant the redundant studs were inclined to try it on occasionally by leaning on the rickety fence and munching on mum's prize-winning azaleas. Each time it happened Ned would get a rocket and a lecture on how to fix the bloody fence.

And there seemed to be a process of sensitisation going on, 'cause each successive rocket took off with more vigour, shall we say. Naturally, Ned, suddenly re-activated from the previous bollocking, would look to kick the dog or generally pass the blame onto some other animate object.

So, on this particular occasion, having had a *real* rev up, which involved some rather pointed reference to his family's pedigree, Ned grabs the pump-action shotgun and a handful of cartridges and leaps out the door to try

and show he was equally upset. At the top of his voice he bellows, 'G'arn you bastards, get the fek out of here. If I catch you here again I'll bloody well castrate you black bastards and nail your nuts to the woolshed wall!' Boom, boom. 'Fek off!' Boom, boom, boom.

At that self-same moment, unbeknownst to Ned, a half-dozen local Maori were in the bull paddock just below the house picking watercress from the main drain, as they often did. It was months before the local grapevine alerted Ned as to why they had bolted out of the paddock and screamed off up the road in their car, vowing never to return.

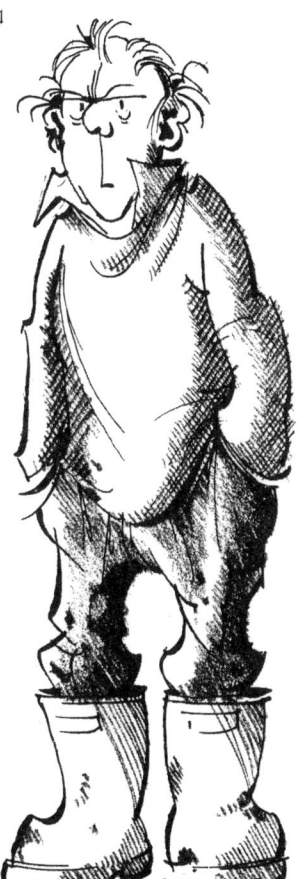

15 Never Lie to Your Insurance Company

Until the introduction of the Environmental Risk Management Authority (ERMA) in 1998, the regular use of explosives without any license or training on farms was a 'customary practice.' One simply wandered into the Stock and Station Agent and collected a bag of detonators and gelignite (or in earlier years one simply dug into a sack of Black Powder for what was required) and shoved them in the back seat of the car with the kids 'n groceries and stuff. In the 1980s and 1990s things were tightened up considerably – you then had to sign for the supplies, but apart from that it was business as usual. Today, it's training courses and licences, dangerous goods stores, inspectors and records, and all sorts of shit. And certainly no more Guy Fawkes party tricks or fishing expeditions or blowing up letter boxes!

This is a yarn about the self-taught Te Kowhai master-blaster and how he came to be drawing a concrete water-tank on his explosives box – you know, like the victory symbols that fighter aces paint on their aircraft after they make a kill.

Peter Rabbit, as he was called locally (and it is probably wise not to speculate on the origins of the nickname),

was determined to remove a table-top-sized willow stump which was in the way of his planned extension to the cow yard. And so he called the local master-blaster in to give the stump the big heave-ho.

Peter farmed in 'Lifestyle Valley' and was completely surrounded by small blocks of urban-escapees. In the master-blaster's opinion (even self-taught as he was) the five houses and a few other out-buildings within a 400-metre radius of the aforementioned tree stump was pushing the odds on an incident-free event a tad. And that's without taking into account Peter's immediately adjacent cowshed, fuel drums and workshop … and a 5000-gallon concrete water tank beside the vat stand to run the milk cooling system.

Peter was very enthusiastic about the instant solution – and the suggestion that a digger was a less risky proposition was promptly rejected in favour of a more fast-track method of removal.

With the proviso of 'all care and no responsibility', and that 'something's gonna get hurt', the master-blaster agreed to continue and twelve sticks of gelignite (10 for the stump and two for luck) were duly placed in a deep hole dug underneath the huge stump. The 'gelly' was inserted on the cowshed/implement shed/water tank/ fuel tank side of the stump in order to vomit away any 'flyrock' or bits of stump, soil, and any other projectile likely to be in the vicinity of the explosives. By this stage, half the district had come to watch in expectation of some fallout, and their expectations were well and truly met.

Kabooom. As planned, the huge stump just managed to tip out of the hole and over onto its back – absolutely perfect. Except, that is, for the 'bit' on the back corner. This slab broke free and oscillated wildly up into the stratosphere – it sailed up and over the cow yard, over the pit, even over the milk-room. Defying gravity it then somehow shimmied down and around the vat stand, and … **kaboof**, it went straight through the concrete water-tank, turning a 5000-gallon tank into a 700-gallon water trough in a nano-second. Just as easy as topping a hard boiled egg!

The crowd, who had been utterly transfixed by the gyrating log, gave a collective groan as a torrent of water was unleashed from the tank. Peter Rabbit, hands wringing in despair, was unamused when the master-blaster laconically noted that, 'By golly, they don't make water tanks like they used to.'

Fairly soon after the initial shock had worn off, the Rabbit began wringing his hands again about 'how was he going to get a new tank before milking tonight?' and 'who's gonna pay for it?'

The blaster asked, 'You've got insurance haven't you?'

'But what will I tell them?' he replied.

'Never lie to your insurance company, Peter,' the blaster declared solemnly. 'Just tell 'em a willow tree fell on the tank.'

16 Mucker

Shy Daisy was approaching teenage-hood and her older brother decided that the quiet farm girl needed some cultural exposure. So one Saturday night, when their oldies were away on holiday, Daisy was taken to a party in 'the big smoke' – at someone's flash house on Hamilton's River Road.

'Twas a bit of an eye-opener for young Daisy sitting quietly in a corner and taking it all in – masses of booze, elevated testosterone levels and even some clearly oestrogen-enhanced females gyrating around the lounge. All very interesting behaviour and utterly fascinating to a country girl.

Things got really intriguing when one of the party animals, Mucker – a respectable trainee insurance salesman in his day life – took exception to the arrival at the party of an uninvited, greasy, leather-clad biker. In an expression of his dislike to biker gangs in general he quietly slipped outside and dropped his old fella into the petrol tank of the Norton Commando. His aim was to recycle the copious amounts of beer he had consumed into bike fuel and so disable the bike somewhere down the road. Mucker's theory was that a biker would be poor and the level of gas in the petrol tank low. Regrettably his theory was proved wrong – the tank was at high tide.

So Daisy's next cultural exposé was of Mucker racing through the party, broken beer bottle in one hand and … what the hang is THAT in the other. He had inadvertently immersed his genitals into the petrol and in severe pain, had whacked the top off his beer bottle and bolted for the bathroom, pouring beer over his dong (and the lounge floor) on the way. Interesting party trick.

Poor Daisy; this sort of behaviour set the benchmark for her own eventual social 'outing' – with role models like this it's little wonder she became a hoon herself! And today Mucker is a highly respected, suit-wearing businessman about town. Though he does tend to flinch a tad when reminded of the night … and he drives a diesel car.

17 Who's Nuts?

Ray PhD, AbC (hons), a boffin working for the Department of Agriculture, was returning from field work in the Kakapuka Mountain area near Te Awamutu. It had been a day of intense research and of precise, maybe some would say even pedantic, attention to detail, as scientists are wont to do. Anyway, driving back to town in his 1964 Vauxhall Wyvern he got a flatty, right outside the Tokanui Psychiatric Hospital.

Ray pulls off the narrow country road onto the grass verge, between the tarseal and a deep water-filled drain. With precision commensurate with his work, he jacks up the car, removes the driver's-side rear wheel (which is dead flat), and carefully places the four wheel nuts in the hubcap on the road edge – not just thrown in the hubcap or dumped on the ground like you or I would do, but carefully arranged in the hub cap reflecting their original placement to within .0001 thousandths of an inch.

While Ray is doing this, an inmate of the psychiatric facility – all arms and legs – flounders over and drapes himself up against the 2-m high security fence. He watches the tyre changing with studied interest.

As he's about to place the spare wheel back on the axle, Ray suddenly notices an oncoming truck and trailer about to do a damn good job of flattening him and his hubcap. With a frantic leap he jumps off the road and cuts in behind his car, inadvertently kicking the hubcap – complete with all the wheel nuts – into the drain full of dirty water.

Now it's a well-known fact that scientists are too pedantic to swear, and besides Ray had an 'audience', so he uttered a few choice expletives – 'golly' and 'by jove'.

What to do? After some protracted intellectual debate with himself about all the possible options to remedy the crisis, a resigned Ray locks the car and prepares to walk the 10 kilometres to Te Awamutu to try and find a garage that could sell him four new wheel nuts. He also concludes that dinner will be cold by the time he walks to town, back to the car, fixes the tyre and drives home.

As he sets off on foot a voice pipes up through the security fence, 'Ot yu going ta do now mister?'

'I'm walking into Te Awamutu, purchasing four new wheel nuts, walking back and fixing my car,' says Ray.

After a brief pause, the inmate says 'Ell, yu'v three other wheels wiff four nuts on. If'n yu take un nut off each wheel, you'll have four wheels wiff three nuts on each!'

Ray, blown away with the profound logic of this statement, concedes: 'I'm not sure, but I think we're both on the wrong side of the fence.'

18 Donkey Business

A well-known and very successful thoroughbred breeder, let's call him John, decided to widen his interests a little and play around with breeding donkeys. Not a big market, he observed, as prices for donkeys came nowhere near the sort of dollar figures he was used to, but, he thought, it could be fun. Donkeys were, after all, almost horses, and their obvious strength of character would present a new challenge.

So John checked out all the technical stuff, and he fenced off a couple of special paddocks, laid on water, built a little barn, a couple of pens, and planted shelter. Soon he was ready for the most important purchase – a well-bred sire. After numerous forays into the market, he got what he wanted and the number one donkey arrived in a modified horse float. A missus for him could follow after he'd settled in.

John did, of course, talk a fair bit about his new pride and joy, and the thoroughbred community that he moved in followed his progress with interest. It was, of course, common knowledge that he'd probably lost his marbles, but everyone was going to enjoy it.

Then his mate Robbie noticed John had suddenly dropped the subject.

'How's y'donkey going?' he enquired.

'Not too damn good,' said John. 'He died … cost me a bloody fortune and now they want a thousand dollars to get rid of 'im … dunno quite what to do, he's just lyin' there, dead.'

Robbie, being a bloke of kind disposition, came to his rescue and offered to take the body off his hands and dispose of him at no cost. He turned up the next morning, rolled the donkey onto the trailer, and John's donkey breeding aspirations and the problems associated with it were resolved, at least for the moment.

A couple of months later John met Robbie again at the club.

'How'd y'get on with that donkey?' he asked. 'I was pretty damn pleased that you took 'im off my hands … What did you do with him?'

'Oh, I raffled him,' said Robbie. 'Charged five bucks a ticket – after all, he was a thoroughbred. Collected three-and-a-half thousand dollars.'

'But, he was bloody dead!' replied John in some confusion. 'What did the poor sod who won him say?'

'Well, quite a bit really,' conceded Robbie. 'He was pretty brassed off, but I sorted him out alright. Gave him his money back … all five dollars of it. There were no hard feelings.'

19 Keste

Keste was a gentleman – he was also argumentative, highly opinionated and usually right. He was what the locals would call 'a clever bastard' and on that score they were right too. He was also a very good farmer.

With advancing age he developed a hobby which he had quietly, and sometimes not so quietly, nurtured over the years. He liked to get stuck into the plonk: whisky, gin, a good brandy and, if they were not immediately available, pretty much anything would do as long as it was alcoholic. It got to be a problem. No surprise in that, but with Keste it got to be a *real* problem.

His partner of the time took it on as her mission to solve the problem, and restore this strong, energetic and talented man to good health. So, she confiscated all the booze. 'What a bugger,' says Keste, as he hops in the car down to the district pub to fill himself up and restock.

So she confiscates the car keys. So he goes in the truck. So she nobbles the truck keys. So he goes down on the tractor. So she hides those keys too. Keste, no doubt, could see the writing on the wall.

Yet somehow Keste still periodically showed up plastered – without having left the farm. Turns out he'd anticipated this developing situation and, as any good strategist would, he'd stashed a pretty good emergency supply at convenient locations around the farm. When the desire for a wee drop became pressing he just remembered something he had to do 'out the back' and went and filled up. Water troughs were a favourite spot; hard for anyone else to locate, safe from being trampled on and, very importantly, cool.

The opposition was, however, tough and committed. One by one she found his hiding places, or at least she found the ones he hadn't drunk yet. And so Keste's supply gradually diminished.

The locals down at the pub followed the deepening crisis with interest and it was suspected a few of them found excuses to call out at the farm and drop off a few bottles, which were promptly stashed in new secret places. It was also suspected that Keste was actually enjoying the battle of wits despite the awful down side of potentially running out entirely.

But it can never be said that Keste gave up easily. Late one afternoon as the locals gathered at the pub for their periodic tipple and a yarn, they looked up to see Keste arriving triumphantly with arm raised high in salute … on his ride-on mower.

20 The Vicar of Tamahere

While the singing in the Waingaro church was often complimented for its enthusiasm, it did receive some criticism for its tone, or lack of it, and the regular distraction of the congregation during the course of many of the hymns.

It wasn't the voices that were the problem, and although the church organ wasn't too crash-hot after its many years of service, they could live with that. The problem was that all the playing and singing woke the possums living in the roof.

When this happened, the scampering around that went on, and the noisy confrontations that invariably accompanied it, shattered the peace and dignity of the place, and the minds of those in the congregation clearly departed to places that the vicar preferred they would not.

In the normal course of time there was an inter-denominational meeting in town and the various issues and problems that the local churches experienced were discussed. Waingaro did not have a resident vicar and relied on a bloke from Ngaruawahia to maintain regular services. In order to promote the local word, Waingaro sent one of their lay preachers to the meeting.

'We've got a big problem,' he announced. 'Possums. They live in the roof of our church and create mayhem when we wake 'em up on a Sunday morning. We tried a pest exterminator but that didn't work.'

The meeting greeted this revelation with some caution, but the preacher persisted.

'We've gotta bloke down the road who knows about possums and he's offered to lay a bit of cyanide or some traps but we're a bit reluctant to go that way.'

So was the meeting. Luckily, the Catholic priest from Huntly came to the rescue with a suggestion. 'I will conduct an exorcism there and that'll put 'em off.'

Well, he did, but they didn't leave.

Another month or two went by and another meeting was held where this ongoing problem was restated. This time a minister from further north, at Onewhero, who'd had some experience in the wider world, said: 'I knew I'd be needed eventually … I'll bring down a group of my parishioners and we will do a group chant. They will leave. Have faith.'

Again, it had no effect whatsoever.

At the next meeting a preacher from town volunteered the services of a gospel choir and while some said it was

A country church.

DAVID HENSHAW.

very good others argued it would drive anything away and was worth a try.

The walls of the little church positively vibrated with song but later there was a rumour that the possums thoroughly enjoyed it and, someone said, that the following Sunday they were already awake when the service began, waiting in anticipation.

Finally, when desperate times demanded desperate measures, something seriously worthwhile needed to be done. The lady vicar from Tamahere stood up and said, 'I could be driving near there next week and I could pop in and have a little chat with them.'

The following week, she picked up the Bishop as she left town. Their visit to Waingaro church was relatively brief, and her response to the situation simple and meaningful. She pulled out the church ladder, poked it through the hatch in the ceiling and ushered up the Bishop. Then she joined him. They both had a few words to say and they left calm and confident.

The next day the possums had gone. The church was quiet and peaceful. The locals made periodic visits to confirm the truth of it. A month later it remained so and enquiries were made.

'What did you do? What did you say?'

'Well,' she quietly replied, 'we treated them like parishioners. We baptised them, we confirmed them all as worthy members of our church, and … well … we haven't seen them since!'

21 Doris's Revenge

You know, they tell me that after many years of wedded bliss the relationship matures from 'anywhere sex' to 'bedroom (only) sex' and eventually to 'hall sex'. The early-marriage sex is self-explanatory (it happens everywhere, anytime) but apparently hall sex is where after decades of living together partners pass each other down the passage and snarl '@#!% you!'

So it was with Doris and partner (known as 'Ironsides' behind his back). After fifty years of marriage, it was inevitable that the internecine one-upmanship between two such strong personalities would escalate to general point scoring at any and every opportunity. And Ironsides, a very strong character with old-school values, tended to have a pretty good scorecard (by his reckoning anyway).

One day, Ironsides decided to paint the chimney on their VERY tall two-storey house, situated on top of a prominent hill looking out towards Pirongia. He'd hired a cherry picker and clearly understood the hire company's imperative to turn the petrol tap off when it wasn't being used 'cause the carby flooded. So, after his post-lunch siesta he whirled away up into the heavens on the extended boom to apply the topcoat. However, he couldn't recall whether he'd turned the petrol off or not, so concluded that turning it in the opposite direction from what it was would be a safe bet.

As he swung out on full reach way over the lawn the motor spluttered into silence. Sitting way up high in a tiny plastic box with dead stick controls had a distinctly unnerving effect on his sense of well-being. Somewhat officiously (due to rising nerves) he ordered Doris to 'just turn the bloody gas on and pull-start the bloody motor.' However, his hectoring tone of voice did not help Doris follow his instructions, and indeed only added to her fumbling. After a succession of less than complementary orders bellowed from 'on high' Doris finally retorted, 'If you're so bloody smart, start the thing yourself,' and went inside … until teatime. Game, set and match to Doris!

Ironsides had a great rejoinder when people suggested to him that he should spend his money with phrases like 'You can't take it with you yu know!' and 'It's no use being the richest man in the cemetery!'

'I'll keep me money, thanks, just in case – I've never met anyone yet who can prove that statement is true.'

22 **The Great Depression Comes to Ongarue**

The years of the Great Depression (1929–1933) caused huge financial and social distress on a global scale and resulted in some very tough times in New Zealand. This is a yarn about Paddy – a rugged and hard-working Kiwi of Irish descent – and his heroic efforts to rescue his family from destitution. The setting is remote Ongarue – the backblocks of the King Country and, even today, not an area associated with dairy farming.

Paddy had a rough hill-country farm at Ongarue, running sheep and beef. As a means to financial salvation in the hard times of the early 1930s, he built a small cowshed and 'converted' part of his farm to milking cows. Paddy's neighbour Bernie was the inspiration for this change – he had already converted to dairying and was enthusiastic about his improved financial circumstances.

Bernie had three daughters whose job every night after school was to hand-milk his herd of placid Jersey cows. Now hand-milking was a very physically demanding process and very tedious. The girls were inclined to talk and so to stop them chatting to each other Bernie built his cowshed with three individual bails some 30 feet apart – times were tough and yakking meant wasting time.

However, rather than buying nice, placid Jersey cows like his neighbour, Paddy economized and roped in some of his Polled Angus beef cows (or 'poleys' as farmers called them). And that is *literally* roped them in! These were wild-run cattle that were content to graze the rough cut-over forest backblock hills largely unmolested by mankind apart from an annual muster – and that event involved happenings not likely to endear mankind to cows. Things like castrations, earmarks, removal of calves and mobs of biting dogs. On being forced into close proximity to people, a 'poley' cow generally becomes aggressive; woe betide any dog or person that comes near her offspring – she instantly turned into a bellowing, slobbering, side-heaving half-ton monster.

To become a dairy farmer, Paddy and his pack of dogs managed to cut thirty 'poley' cows and their calves out of the bush and coerce them home to the front paddock. Thereafter, each morning he used to muster the reluctant mob into the yards to segregate the calves from their mums. This was to allow his 'dairy' cows to 'bag up' so he could harvest their milk later that evening.

Milking each reluctant cow became an epic battle.

Paddy was forced to rig up a sturdy block and tackle in front of the bail – to get a cow in to be hand-milked he first had to lasso one of the wild critters in the yard and then winch the unwilling donor into the bail. All that agro was accompanied by a chorus of encouragement from his mongrel dogs through the rails, and the mutts' enthusiasm for the battle only heightened as Paddy approached the intimate parts of the now hog-tied beast to relieve her of her miserable pint or two of milk.

After what must have been a truly terrible month or so someone asked him, 'How is the dairying venture going Paddy?'

'Oh begorra', 'tis not too bad, not too bad,' says Paddy in a gross understatement of the rodeo at milking time. 'One or two of the cows even come into the bail on their own now.'

After milking, Paddy used to cart his precious now-separated cream to the neighbour's to be collected for processing into butter at the Taumarunui Dairy Factory. This transportation was done by placing the tall cream cans in his old wooden wheel barrow and trundling them along the track a mile down the way. However, this top-heavy load proved to be prone to overturning – with the resultant loss of his hard-won income. So he modified an old horse harness and would hitch 'mum' up to pull the heavy barrow down the road loaded with cream cans while he steadied the contraption from behind.

These years in Ongarue were no doubt tough times indeed for men, women and children. However, there was also one mob of poley cows that used to look longingly through the barbed wire fence at the scrub and bush on the hills, also hoping, no doubt, for a rapid end to the Great Depression.

23 The Day It Rained Geese

Way back in 1905, the North American Canadian goose was brought into the country by the Acclimatisation Society – the parent of today's Fish and Game Council. It was just one of many so-called 'beneficial' game and fur animals that were imported into New Zealand over the decades – other 'winners' included ferrets, stoats, weasels, possums, mynas, deer …

A hundred years on from their release, farmers and croppers in many parts of New Zealand are seriously angry at what these birds get up to. In fact, they hate 'Canadas' with a passion, calling them the 'grubby goose' or 'flying rabbit' – they can behave like a mob of grass-eating, ground-hopping vermin but are twenty times more cunning than a plague of bunnies. Two or three geese appear to be able to eat the equivalent of what one sheep consumes daily.

A mob of 2000 geese – not uncommon down south – consumes massive amounts of forage and can eject about 700 kilos of excrement per day, spoiling pasture and fouling waterways.

Considerable pressure is put on the government to get the Canada goose removed from the protection of the Wildlife Act and rescheduled a pest. With luck, they'll be tagged 'shoot on sight' *instead of being protected as gamebirds for the hunting elite during the shooting season.*

Athol of Rotokauri developed a real hatred of Canada geese and he had damn good cause. Around 1970, the Acclimatisation Society, bless their souls, had introduced some geese from the South Island into the private wildlife park owned by Murray Powell near Hamilton.

After considerable and somewhat heated debate with the local branch of Federated Farmers about the unwelcome potential of the geese, the Society had settled with an agreement (sworn-under-oath-on-the-Bible-so-help-me-God-type promise) that they would only *ever* keep a maximum of 16 geese, and that they would be pinioned – a surgical process undertaken to stop birds flying. Some agreement! The pinioned birds laid prolific numbers of non-pinioned eggs and nobody got round to docking the chicks. Before you could blink, there were gaggles of geese galore – whole flocks of the so-called flightless fowl were migrating out of the wildlife park onto surrounding farmland.

If you're thinking so much as a smile, just remember that I have your face burned in my memory an' next May you'll be in deep trouble!

Maungatautari with Lake Karapiro in the foreground.

According to Murray, who annually raised and sold pheasants to the Society and who sympathised with the farmers' concerns, the emerging successor to the Acclimatisation Society, the Fish and Game Council not only reneged on their promise but 'burnt the bible they swore on as well.'

Murray had been an active member of both organisations for 50 years and states that the emerging 'Fish 'n Game just ran over the top of the local farmers.' And, while they waffled, the geese continued to fly and breed and graze and shit.

Athol tried about every trick in the book to discourage the '16-going-on-100 flightless' birds that flew into his paddocks from the wildlife park. He learned that somehow the moment he opened the gun-rack the flock took to the air. He tried gin traps. He tried straw dummies and flappers on the fence but all he learnt was that the goose is extremely cunning. One day he heard a rumour from the South Island that the ectoparasiticide Warbex – licensed to treat lice on cattle – was lethal on geese, so effective that they became 'stone dead in two minutes flat.' So he treated a sack of wheat, baited the paddock and sat back to await his day of revenge. And he literally sat back – in a deck chair, beer in one hand and a stopwatch in the other. The *finale* involved firing up the Fergie at two-and-a-bit minutes and sneaking a whole tractor load of dead geese down to bury in the offal hole. Gone. Vanished. Geeseless!

Unfortunately, a neighbour drove up for a visit and the wily mob took to the air – at 1 minute 45 seconds. And I'll tell you what those wily bloody geese can cover a hell of a lot of territory when they are spooked. In Rotokauri and Whatawhata and Te Rapa the old-timers still talk about the mystery of the day it rained dead geese!

Not all the Acclimatisation Society's gamebirds were so unwelcome. Murray Powell, the well-known founder of what has now become the Hamilton Zoo, used to breed around 17,000 pheasants each year at Rotokauri as a gamebird. The local Acclimatisation Society would purchase the hen and cock pheasants to restock prime hunting areas around the greater Waikato with money obtained from shooting licences. The Society would drive down country roads releasing the gamebirds in areas which showed good pheasant habitat or if the local grapevine was working well, where a farmer just happened to be at the letterbox with a crate of beer. Particular largesse was bestowed on any farm that allowed a member of the 'hook and bullet brigade' (today's nickname for members of Fish and Game) to have shooting access.

Over in the Karakariki Valley, Jimmy Johnson's dad was an avid 'rooster' hunter on his own farm. When he observed the Acclimatisation chaps driving slowly up the long valley releasing the odd bird he seized the opportunity to enhance the next shooting season.

A hearty hello and 'how about a cuppa you guys' were issued to the release team and the pre-programmed young Jimmy was told to 'git outside and play.' Mysteriously, during that very affable afternoon tea break, the pin in the pheasant cage came out and the door slid itself open. Whoof, 600 cock pheasants lit out!

After the congenial brew, the Acclimatisation guys went back to their vehicle and seeing the empty trailer cage realised they'd been totally had.

Little Jimmy was most conspicuous by his absence and, despite the hook and bullet brigade's evident anger, his dad was unable to avoid a smug expression. Indeed, young Jimmy was a hero in the valley for quite a few years.

24 **Of Flys and Flies**

Noel Stack of Thames and his brother-in-law Ian were natural pranksters. Like many seasoned 'winder-uppers' they didn't really have to set out to create amusement, they simply grabbed the opportunity as it came along. So it was in the Te Puru pub that after having a few glasses before 'Six O'clock Closing' Noel headed off to the toilet. The local drunk, 'three sheets to the wind' as usual, was in there fumbling around with his crotch at the urinal.

Noel says, 'Wha'sa matter Tom?'

'Can't get me bloody flies done up,' slurred a thoroughly pissed Tom (this was in the days before zippers).

Noel, seizing the opportunity, offers to assist Tom. Grabbing the sleeve of Tom's navvy jacket, he buttons the cuff of one arm to Tom's crotch.

'There you are mate, you're right now,' says Noel, and nips back to the bar to tell all his cobbers about what he's done.

They aren't disappointed. After some time Tom staggers out into the bar, one arm crooked across his front and one arm waving wildly, shrieking, 'I'm buggered. I've had a stroke. I'M PARALYSED.'

Noel and crew were just about paralytic themselves … from laughter at Tom's expense.

——— *** ———

In the days before urban wastewater (sewer) systems and flushing inside toilets, each home had an outside loo or 'night closet'. This was different to the rural version – the 'long drop' or 'the dunny'. Under the 'townie' toilet seat was a removable drum which the night-cart operator removed and swapped with an empty can. The man would arrive under cover of darkness and remove the family's business for disposal. This 'treatment' of bodily waste was, as it is today, a sort of out-of-sight out-of-mind process where everyone knew what happened but nobody 'noticed'.

Noel and Ian turned their humorous attentions to publicising the 'night soil' story. One night, Noel

and brother-in law Ian undid the wheel nuts almost completely on the night cart while the chap was collecting the next batch of 'goods'. You can guess the result when the night cart man hopped on, shook the reins and said 'Gee up.'

The next morning the community could not help but acknowledge the night-cart man and his unpleasant but necessary job – the discreet removal of large quantities of wees and poos had become everybody's business that morning. It was all over the road, with the hapless driver trying to shovel up the mess.

Noel and Ian also caught out another night-cart man. This one had a leather apron which went over his shoulders to protect him from the edges of the dunny can, and to deflect any splashes should they occur. While having a few beers at the pub, Noel and co. had observed the chap going into a house through a gap in the hedge out the back. They waited until he was swapping cans and strung a length of No. 8 wire across the gap at ankle height. Talk about leaving the piss and getting on the hard stuff!

25 A Big Wedding

It was indeed a big wedding. There was a marquee in the expansive garden with garden seats, trestle tables and flowers all over the place. Cars were parked in the paddocks, and there was a well-stocked play area for the children to keep them occupied and out of the way of the main event.

John went. Not because he particularly wanted to but because there were expectations that he should. And, he reasoned, there would be a big spread, heaps of free plonk and, most importantly, a fair few of his mates.

It was all very grand and filled with good humour and best wishes and the *bonhomie* that goes with such an occasion. John got full of food, full of booze, kissed the bride, shook the groom by the hand, and settled down with more food, more booze and his mates to re-organise the way the country was run.

It was all quite idyllic but for one small complication. One of the lady guests had an acute dislike of John. It didn't worry him too much as he reflected that she was entitled to her opinion – he didn't like her much either, but whatever, 'live and let live'.

As the afternoon wore on, however, she kept noisily expressing her opinions and found in her vocabulary some colourful and uncomplimentary words to explain what a bad man he was, and why quite simply he should not even be there. There was one trait of John's that she did overlook, and it was perhaps the one that best described his personality … mischievous.

John had preserved his silence, as he reasoned any gentleman would, and he was, after all, a gentleman. But lady, you're pushing it.

The chance for retribution arose when she went for a walk in the sprawling gardens and left her camera on one of the garden seats. John spotted the opportunity. He casually strolled past the seat, gathered up the camera and disappeared into the nearby shrubbery. There he handed the camera to a mate, dropped his pants and got his friend to take a few good close-up shots of his private bits. Then he quietly and unobtrusively returned the camera to the garden seat.

The action was deemed discreet and highly successful and John basked in the eventual outcome when the film was developed. It would all be immensely satisfying and the reactions dramatic to say the least. There, among the photographs of the bride and the groom, the cake and the garden would be 'this'. Shock, horror, how did that

Woodlands Homestead, Gordonton.

get there? Yes, indeed, very satisfying and the photo shop she went to back home would have a field day when they developed the film.

It is said, that later there emerged something of a 'technical hitch'. The bloke who took the shots aimed a wee bit high and had picked up the bottom of John's tie. Some astute detective work followed and the lady was able to identify who had been wearing that tie.

The mischief was revealed, along with other things! Whoops!

26 King Country Kung Fu

Everyone agreed Felix was a gun fencer, one of the King Country's best. One day, he was constructing a new fence on a block near the 'Eight Mile Junction' – the intersection eight miles out of Te Kuiti where the roads head south to New Plymouth and Taumarunui. Nearby, his employer, Rob, a bunch of kids and a couple of useless dogs were trying to muster a mob of 'bolting bloody lambs' for docking, with a remarkable lack of success.

Out of the kindness of his heart, Felix dropped his fencing gear and rushed over to help. At the same time, Rob – by now totally frustrated with both the lambs and with one dog that had an uncanny ability to be in the wrong place at the right time – grabbed a large stick to heave at the dog, in the hope of encouraging a more helpful attitude. As he wildly flung his arm back to throw, half the branch broke away and went sailing off behind him.

Now one of Murphy's Laws states, 'no good deed goes unpunished' and so Felix's headlong rush to help and the branch's vigorous arc were unfortunately destined to intersect. The result: Felix's teeth (luckily, false) were smashed in.

He leapt up, spat out his broken teeth and roared, 'What kung fu that bloody stick!' And so the King Country can, perhaps, lay claim to its own particular brand of that ancient martial art.

27 Next Time Hire a Chimney Sweep

She was a big lady; intimidating, short-tempered and not shy in her choice of expletives when she wanted something done and pronto. He, on the other hand, was a little bloke. And, not surprisingly, was very much inclined to comply with instructions whenever they were given and whatever they involved.

'Chimney needs cleaning,' she announced one day. 'Get up there and get on with it. And I want it done properly, mind. Get a rope, and a sack, and tie it all up tight, and wrap some barbed wire around the sack, and just get on with it.'

And so he duly made the preparations and climbed onto the roof. The chimney-cleaning operation was due to commence, and as he dropped the sack down the chimney he yelled down the hole at the top of his voice, 'Look out!'

The reaction from below was swift and noisy. Before the echo had even died away, she exploded out the front door angry and abusive and, rather significantly, covered in soot.

'You stupid […]! Why didn't you warn me?'

'I did,' he innocently replied. 'I said "look out".'

'You third-rate, ignorant, dopey, thoughtless […] – you said "look up"!'

28 There's No Flies on My Mum!

Like many folk, William's mum was a regular church-goer. Every Sunday morning she would 'flash up' and head off to church. As a seven-year-old this routine was something of a mystery – all that fluffing around with the hair and good clothes to go and listen to someone talk about some mysterious and nebulous person or thing called 'God'. So, one day he 'substituted' Mum's hair spray for a can of fly spray by swapping the lids. Mum got all dressed up and then having done the usual coiffure job proceeded to set the style with 'hair spray'.

The trick worked perfectly, but William made two basic mistakes. One, he stuck around to watch the results and two, he then compounded the error by saying, 'There's no flies on my mum.'

His normally mild mother would have definitely needed to seek forgiveness from the Lord that morning, and William found sitting down a fairly delicate process for a day or two.

29 Hoddle

Ken Hoddle was a well-known Waikato character. He grew up in the backblocks of the King Country and eventually ended up in Horotiu selling second-hand tractors and tractor parts. His mischievous outlook on life can be illustrated by his response when farmers would complain about the price of his parts: 'I have not increased my prices in 20 years – I have always only ever charged half of new price.'

Late one Saturday night, a young hoon insisted on doing wheelies up and down the street where Ken lived – possibly trying to send a Michelin mating call to a certain young lady. Eventually, the neighbourhood wearied of the constant engine revving and squealing tyre noises. Many were annoyed to the point of wakefulness, but beyond peering out from curtains and grumbling the community put up with the unwelcome nocturnal visitor. Eventually the young fella cut short his demonstration by running out of gas. He legged it off towards Ngaruawahia for a refill in anticipation of continuing his serenade. Ken, in his usual direct way, acted. Well, that is the speculation and as Ken is no longer with us that is how it will have to remain.

So, while the driver was away *someone* picked the errant car up on a forklift and deposited it on top of a bus shelter. Thus it appeared the next day on the front page of the *Waikato Times* – a photo of a car hanging off the roof looking like a beached whale.

Mr Policeman duly undertook many interviews in the neighbourhood as to how such a mystery could have happened, but the neighbours, without exception, had not been aware of any vehicle noises during the night, let alone known how some sort of large 'lifting device' could have possibly picked up the car without them hearing it.

The moonstruck (or was it dumbstruck) young man had to hire a crane to retrieve his car.

One day, Hoddle paid a visit to his tractor wrecker's yard. Now this acre-or-three of dead and dying tractors had the outward appearance of a real mess but Hoddle knew where every nut and bolt was. One day he received an unsolicited visit from an overly zealous Waipa County Inspector. He worked his way around the yard criticising anything he could in an effort to exert his authority. Unusually, Ken was not argumentative, but agreed with everything the inspector said.

Eventually they were standing by the main gate set within the high security fence that surrounded the property. They continued to talk, and Ken continued to agree with the nit-picking inspector. Then Ken stepped out onto the verge, pulled the gate to, snipped the padlock and walked off. He said over his shoulder, 'Yur doin a good job. I'm off to lunch – you help yourself to the yard. Look at anything you like,' leaving the county guy locked INSIDE the dismantling yard. It was a very long lunch break for both parties.

30 **Maggot Pies**

Country stores are wonderful inventions. Whether you run out of baking soda or bread, or 2-inch post staples for that matter, you can just nip down to the local store. Out of necessity, the range of merchandise is far wider than your typical city dairy. As a consequence, some items have rather an extended shelf life – and 'use by' dates can be interpreted fairly liberally.

Rev's family, at Te Rahu near Te Awamutu, feeling the need for a Sunday lunch treat, sent young Steven down to the local to grab a meat pie for each of the mob. Being a typical hungry-gutted teenager, Steven scoffed his on the way home in about three big bites – a bit like a gannet glugging down a fish really. The rest of the family, being more restrained, put their pies on plates and gathered knives and forks and sat at the table. One of Steve's siblings peeled back the lid to apply 'tucker stuffer' (aka tomato sauce) and exclaimed:

'Ooh, this pie has rice in it. I hate rice.'

Uh oh …

'Mum, MUM the rice is moving! IT'S MAGGOTS!'

By now Steve's Adam's apple is bouncing around like a bungy-jumper as he tries to put on a brave face in the midst of general hilarity.

31 The Power of Multiplication

This story bears some resemblance to Bryce Courtenay's book The Power of One *– only instead of Peekay it involves another kid who learnt early that the power of two was a hell of a lot better.*

Growing up in a rural community in the Waikato during the 1960s was as good as it got. I poached my first rabbit at seven with a single-shot Savage rifle and had grown into my own double-barrelled shotgun by 11 – which I promptly 'blooded' by winging my elderly duck-shooting partner with several (nearly) spent ricochet pellets. Life was all about 'hunt'n and fish'n'. Weekends and evenings involved roaming over huge areas of farm and bush – much of which became more accessible from a homemade canoe. Summer was bliss, with freedom to explore and wander and swim in the Waipa River whenever I felt inclined. The only dark cloud in my life was that somewhere in the equation there was a distraction called school.

Anyway I digress. Sitting in the mai mai shooting ducks with Mr. Effingham Robson from Hopuhopu (always Eff to the young me) I got to listen to all sorts of yarns. One slow, wet day Eff told me about Tui, the Maori joker he shore sheep with who was way smarter than the local council. To make the story even more appealing, it involved my pet hate – maths.

As part of its responsibilities for pest control, the Waipa County Council used to swap either bullets (4 x .22 calibre rifle or 1 shotgun shell) for a rabbit tail or cash for polecat/ferret tails (5 shillings) and for pairs of harrier hawk legs (2/6d). Now that doesn't sound like much sponduli but it kept Tui in ammunition and cash.

So whenever Eff's mate Tui killed a polecat, he cut off the tail and posted it to the council to claim the bounty. Here's the kicker that appealed to me – rather than just snip off the tail he made sure he included a good chunk of 'back steak' and then snipped the tail in half. He packaged up the bits, addressed it to the County Council and put his return details on the back, along with the declaration that it contained *two* ferret tails. He then left the open parcel on a fence post for a couple of days and let the maggots get stuck in. Into the post it went and by the time the box was finally dumped on the Pest Officer's desk it was fair oozing – he'd read the sender details, open the box, get a whiff of rotten meat, go, 'One tail, two tails' and slam it in the rubbish bin. To a nine-year-old suddenly the logic of maths had a damn useful application – 1 tail becomes 2 and 5 shillings becomes 10 shillings. Hmmm, thinks I.

Anyway Eff's mate also had this pet ferret he used to chase rabbits out of their warrens. He would net the bolting rabbits and take their tails for bounty or the carcasses to eat. One day the 'best ferret in the world' caught a rabbit, had a feed down the burrow and went to sleep. Tui put his arm down the burrow to drag out the pet polecat and it bit right through his thumb. It defied any attempts to prise its mouth open and with tears in his eyes he got Eff to kill it and cut off its teeth with a hacksaw. However, the physical pain was ameliorated somewhat by ripping the county off for ten bob.

Now at the time Eff told me this yarn I had a box of 227 rabbit and hare tails. So that was … 227 times 4 bullets which equals…um, a damn lot of fun. What about 227 tails divided (as in cut) in two, multiplied by 4 bullets? Man that's a whole load of action. This division and multiplication business had opened up a whole new world since that mai mai conversation.

I sorted out all the big tails (a few tails were from kits pulled from the burrow and were very small) and snipped them in two. The massive hare tails were good for three cuts. After some strategic thinking, I rang the Pest Officer with a request that he call in and uplift my 'hundreds and hundreds of tails' (thereby cunningly preconditioning him) and hand over the bounty. Having organised it for when my parents were absent (they would have been shocked to know about my passion for the power of two – in fact I probably would have got my butt thrashed) and putting on my 'thoughtful and innocent look' the visit went like this:

'Hey, you're only a kid.'

'Yes sir, I am just a bit small for my age, but, well a rabbit tail is a bounty tail, and there's nothing in the book that says they have to be shot by someone of a particular age. After all I'm doing the County a favour by removing lots of noxious pests.' (I'd actually *studied* for this – I'd read up on pest management so I could sound plausible.)

'Well, hang, I suppose so. Let's have a look at all these tails. Crikey kid, you weren't joking when you said you had hundreds.'

'Now sir, some of these are a bit small – they've been taken from lots of young rabbits,' I say as I'm running bits of fluff past him like a conjuror shuffling cards.

'You're not kidding – you must have the County's smallest rabbits. And some of them are pretty damn ripe!' (Oops, too many rotten rabbit back steaks included in the mix, *à la* Tui).

'Look sir, my hands are already dirty and smelly from showing these to you. How about you watch and I'll count them for you – there are exactly 454 bounty tails here or 20.2 boxes of ammunition.'

'That's a good idea kid. On second thoughts, how about I just give you 15 boxes of ammo and we call it quits?'

'Oh okay.' (Yesss!)

'Chuck the box of tails in the back of my vehicle and I'll burn it all when I get back to work.'

And so my aversion to scholastic activity completely abated thanks to a yarn in a duck shooting mai mai.

I had finally learnt the usefulness of knowing how to divide and multiply – and that philosophy still applied when I eventually transferred my mathematical enthusiasm from rabbits to girls – divide 'em out of the mob …

32 Diarrhoea Dialogue

George of Maihihi had little need for officious bastards or people trying to rule his life. Thus, when he was on the receiving end of a very pedantic and argumentative Insurance Assessor who was trying to weasel his way out of paying a claim, George thought 'don't get mad – get even.' Therefore after weeks of acrimonious debate over the phone George insisted the Assessor come to visit and sort this out (meaning he was going to agree with George's claim). As part of the consensus the Assessor was going to reach (only

he didn't now this yet), George offered the chap a nice hot cup of tea and a scone. The beverage was however liberally doped with a strong and fast-acting laxative. To allow the concoction time to work George embarked upon a protracted discussion about the affairs of the world and the weather and the merits of every horse in the Melbourne Cup and the bloody politicians. All quite affable.

Meanwhile the Assessor was becoming aware that something very unusual was happening in his guts as the laxative began to make its presence felt. Still unaware that he had been nobbled, the agent began to realise all was not well 'down below' and increasingly began to cast covert looks for the location of the loo. Finally, nearing desperation, he asked to use the little room. A forthright George replied, 'No way are you going to use my toilet until we sort out this insurance claim.' After all the weeks of debating, the claim was signed off in about 20 seconds flat!

33 Care With the Shottie Mate

Kevin had a place over the other side of the Waipa. He'd lived there for years and the children had grown up and found their own lives, leaving Mum and Dad to quietly go on farming and pretty much enjoy themselves. Advancing years were, however, causing the old boy a few problems, which had persisted to the extent that he felt obliged to do the one thing he'd always steadfastly resisted – talk to his local doctor.

He was embarrassed and skirted around the issue, reasoning that the Doc would work out what he meant.

'Got a bit of a problem Doc,' he said. 'Down below.'

Further explanation followed. 'A bit like an old dog really … I tell him to "get in behind" and he won't, and I tell 'im to "get away out" and he won't … y'know what I mean. It's all getting a bit difficult an' it slacks me off an' my wife's not too keen on it either.'

The Doc looked suitably caring and understanding. 'There's nothing unusual in this mate, you just need not to get too anxious.' Of course, the Doc understood that as age crept up the problem inevitably emerged for most men. 'I'm going to refer you to a psychiatrist friend of mine who'll be just the ticket.'

Now it was pretty much an established fact that those sort of blokes were not Kevin's cup of tea, but neither was the complete absence of a sex life. So, reluctantly, he kept the appointment. To his immense relief he quickly realised that the psychiatrist was a very practical sort of bloke who didn't muck about. 'Look mate,' he said, 'what you need is a kick start. Get the adrenalin running. Stick your shotgun under the bed and load it, one shell, and just a blank, will do. Now next time you and your missus are building up a head of steam and you're getting a bit anxious, just reach under the bed an' pull the trigger. It'll make a helluva noise and charge up your adrenalin and you'll be away. Trust me.'

Kevin could see the logic in this and returned home with a spring in his step.

Several weeks later he was back for a routine follow-up, and he was looking a bit worse for wear.

'How'd it go?' asked the psychiatrist cautiously.

'Well,' said Kevin. 'Not brilliant … I pulled both triggers on the shottie and instantly realised I'd made a couple of mistakes. I'd stuck in two shells instead of one, *and* they were both live. I've only just got my hearing back. I broke my thumb. The missus had a hernia, and the bed collapsed. The next morning I realised there's a bloody great hole in the wall. Most of the windows have gone, and the curtains are a bit stuffed. And my best dog, who was sleeping on the veranda, got shot. I think I'm gonna be single for a while.'

34 The Night Daisy Moved

Mac of Te Pahu had a problem. Daisy, jersey cow number 134, wouldn't move, couldn't move and would never move. She was dead. In fact, by the look of her, she had been dead for a week before she was floated up onto Mac's river flats by yet another flood. But, larger than life and wheezing like suppurating Scottish bagpipes, she HAD to move.

There's an old saying: 'where you have livestock, you're gonna have dead stock.' In days of old, Waikato farmers simply disposed of 'fallen animals' by shoving them into an inconspicuous gully and leaving nature to deal with them. Unfortunately Mac's neighbour's out-of-site out-of-mind gully happened to be adjacent to Mac's house. Summertime found leaving any window open invited a curtain of blowflies into every part of the house, and cooking a roast was only achievable at night when the dirty buggers had gone to bed, or whatever blowies do after hours. Investigations revealed not one but five decomposing animals. The neighbour couldn't understand Mac's agro: 'We don't have any flies at our place!'

Therefore the advent of JD Wallace Ltd's rendering or 'boiling down' plant for 'fallen' bovines (cows) at Waitoa and its dead animal collection service, proved a blessing for farmers throughout the Waikato. Just pick up the phone and their high-sided truck whisked away the carcass. This service recycles: cow hides eventually become leather shoes and carcasses get turned into blood and bone fertiliser for the garden. It was sort of a forerunner of today's 'closed loop' manufacturing ethos.

Anyway, the terribly wet spring of 1979 had really stressed land, people and animals, and the unfortunate 'harvest' of the awful weather had proven too much for the capacity of Wallace's works. They had stopped collecting fallen stock as they had ten acres of Daisy's decomposing mates stacked up in a paddock waiting for the skinners to catch up.

In a normal spring – the peak 'skinning season' – Wallace's hide-removers would hit the Waihou Pub for a beer after a hard day of flaying the hides off the not-so-fresh dead and deceased. Their usual *eau de Waitoa* fragrance was such that they were more than welcome to their end of the bar. However, in the '79 season, in trying to clear the massive backlog, they had the whole pub to themselves and even the barman tried to find urgent work 'out back'.

Suddenly bereft of the rendering plant option, some 'gumboot-dancers' (as Kiwi dairy farmers are nicknamed) resorted to sneaking dead cows into local rivers – sort of like a 'message in a leather bag' to others down stream. In response, the Waikato Regional Council in its theoretical wisdom *insisted* that if one of these dead cows landed on your farm, you had to drag her up to the road to await the resumption of Wallace's collection. Yeah right! Like that's going to happen. Hook up the Fergie and with one yank of the snig chain you'd have a week-old cow going to pieces all over your paddock.

Another one of the endless spring floods of that horrible year had deposited Daisy from somewhere up the Waipa River onto Mac's paddock and there was no way in hell Mac was about to take 'er for a drag through his farm. Desperate times meant desperate measures. Somehow she had to be moved on.

Mmmm, what about some gelignite?

Full moon, dressed up like an Irish bomb disposal squaddy (in case the by-now bloated beast popped), Mac bored a hole in the ground under each end of the carcass, fused 'er up with two plugs of jelly and WHAMMO, off Daisy went.

And boy did she go – through the willows she flew, up and up, end over end, until internal tensions overcame the lift-off boost. The previously Delightful Daisy became Disintegrating Daisy. She rained down all over the river … for miles … floating bits of internal organs, legs, lungs, the works. Not even a hair was left on Mac's farm. Problem solved. Daisy had been moved on. Well, sort of.

A week later, downriver farmers were going absolutely berserk. There'd been another flood and it had spread Daisy over their paddocks all the way down to Ngaruawahia. As Barry at Whatawhata muttered, 'Some bastard must have put bits of a dead beast in the river and my cows are going mental … they've gone right orf their milk.'

Hey diddle diddle
Mac had a fiddle
And the cow jumped over the moon …

35 Penal Rates

It's an unwritten rule in rural New Zealand that you NEVER ring anybody after nine in the evening – unless it's life or death, or you know that person extremely very bloody extra well. Unlike the 'latte set', country folk start early, work hard, and retire at a sensible time.

Footy, a gumboot-dancer, however, was an exception to this first rule of rural etiquette. He'd have a leisurely dinner, read the newspaper from cover to cover, have a yak with Mum, dwell over a cup-o-tea and then … 'Crikey, I must ring Ted and see how his new grass is growing.'

Unfortunately, by 10.35 pm Ted has already stacked up some serious zzzzz's. Totally disorientated by the screaming telephone, he manages to hang onto a subliminal conversation with Footy and then immediately re-submerges into sleep – with no recollection of the event the next morning.

However, this goes on for a bit and becomes something of a regular occurrence. Finally, one morning Ted wakes up with an attitude for who the hell rang last night – again! This was just not on and advice was sought in the community and a strategy was planned. Several ideas were latched onto and Wal and Les were delegated to assist to house train the errant Footy.

Wal's method was explained to Ted.

Wal, a straight shooter who professes to insomnia once woken, advocated a standard reply after 9 pm.

'Ring, Ring Ring Ring'.

Wal: 'Hello. I don't know who the fek you are. I don't know what the fek you want. FEK OFF.' Click!

His theory is that he isn't embarrassed as he doesn't know who woke him, and they never do it again. Too bad if it's the mother in law.

After a number of post-10 pm calls, Les, like Ted was desperate for an idea to sort out the problem. He was the local livestock truckie and these guys also start real early and attempt to finish before dark.

'Yeh Les, Footy here, can you come and pick up two cows for the Frankton Sale in the morning.'

Les: 'Mumble, mumble, mutter. Yeh … Hey, IT IS THE BLOODY MORNING YOU MORON!'

So through Les the district plots utu. He sets the alarm for 3.30 am.

'Yeh Footy, Les here. Listen, I was half asleep when you rang last night and I wasn't sure if you had a cow or a calf to take to Frankton. What'ivugot?'

Footy, 'Mumble mumble … DO YOU KNOW WHAT THE HELL TIME IT IS!?

Les drifts off to sleep with a mile-wide smile.

The Bombay Hills, from the north Waikato.

The booze cost you 40 bucks, the car's worth stuff all, an' you obviously
don't value your life ... but the gate an' 2 strainers will cost you $198.50!

36 Matthew

The lad who worked on Scotty's place had a cavalier disregard for the law and, in particular, for speed limits imposed, he said, 'by suits in Wellington who hadn't got a bloody clue about how fast a car driven by a competent driver could handle a road.'

He saw the signs that said, 'the faster you go the bigger the mess' but didn't read them. Others said, 'Drink, drive, die' and he thought, 'Yeah, sure.'

Someone asked him one day what he did with the time he saved by travelling fast, but it didn't sink in. Going like the clappers was cool, it was fun, his car was a confidence boost, and he had absolute faith in his ability as a driver. He even noticed a slight increase in this faith every time he watched a car rally on TV, or the Indy 500, or if he went over to Morrinsville to the burn-out rally. He saw himself as bullet-proof.

Now it is reasonable to accept that this philosophy is not unique. Any young bloke knows it. And those that don't are old. Poor bastards, he felt sorry for them. The rules and the slogans were all devised by old bastards and there's a lot of old bastards around that have got to do something to make themselves feel useful.

He came down from Auckland one night in an hour twenty.

'That's a bit on the quick side,' said Scotty.

'Sure,' said Matt, proud of it.

'Don't y'know the quicker y'go the bigger the mess?' said Scotty.

'Sure,' said Matthew, and thought what a load of crap.

'We don't want you banged up y'know,' said Scotty. '… y'got a long life ahead of you and we care.'

'Sure,' said Matt.

Clearly the message was not getting through and it became apparent that a different tack was needed if safety was to be preserved and a long life ensue. Scotty had been 22 himself once, and it didn't take a lot of thought to remember what his main objective in life was at that time. Especially, if that main objective was waiting in hot anticipation for him to drive down from Auckland in an hour twenty! So, sort of casually, he said, 'Think what y'might miss out on if you die young.'

'Like what?' says Matt.

'Oh … about 50 years give or take a bit … of sex.'

Suddenly Scotty had Matt's undivided attention.

37 Haybarn Ballet

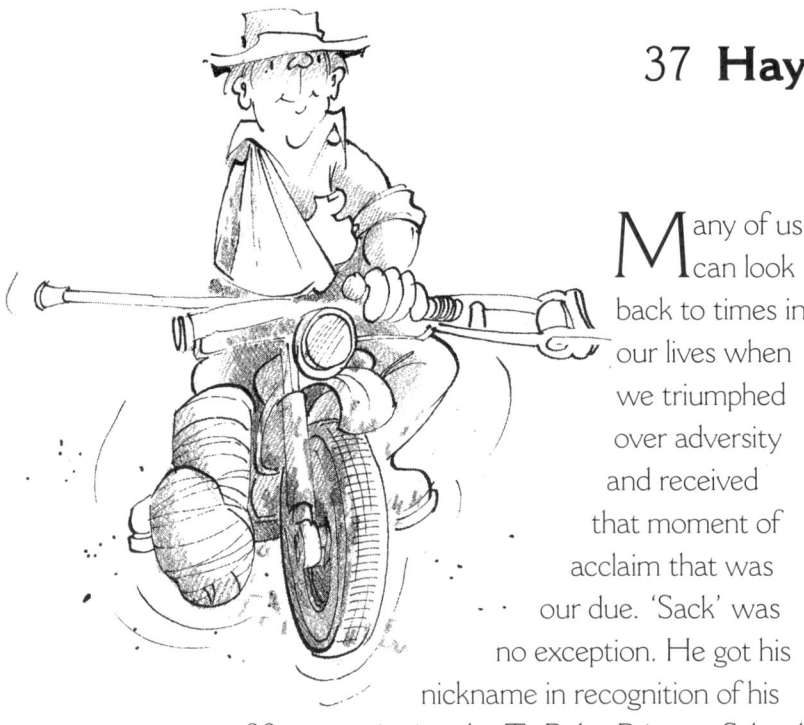

Many of us can look back to times in our lives when we triumphed over adversity and received that moment of acclaim that was our due. 'Sack' was no exception. He got his nickname in recognition of his moment of fame – winning the Te Rahu Primary School under-7s sack race.

He was legendary, too, in his mid-life years for his yen for 'looking over the fence'. If you know what I mean. Perhaps hoping to relive his childhood glory, he was always keen to get in the sack… preferably not his own.

Anyway, living up near Waeranga, his neighbour's missus sort of developed the same inclinations and between them they choreographed a slick routine. Sack would rip across the paddocks on his 2-wheel farm bike,

up and over a pre-placed plank on either side of the boundary fence, into the haybarn and … well, you can figure that one out for yourself. The timing was brilliant. Sack could whip down to lock the cows in, clear the fence at 20 miles an hour and be back home for breakfast before Mum had finished cooking the porridge.

The neighbour's husband eventually wised up to all this overtime his wife was putting in feeding the calves and so one day he decided it was time to 'pull the plank' on the extra-curricular activities, so to speak. Well, Sack hit that non-existent ramp at full gallop, misty eyed and full of anticipation and, in his mind, three steps into the haybarn ballet.

If you can imagine a seven-wire cheese grater in action, you will have some idea of what happened when Sack hit that boundary fence. It sure meddled with the libido a tad! When a battered Sack finally reported in for porridge, he informed the long-suffering missus that he had turned over a new leaf and was going to stick close to home from now on. Prompted by the surprised response, he quite truthfully explained that 'he'd been over-doing it a bit' and had finally 'hit the wire'.

38 Early Teaching Days in the Waikato

Huntly in the early 1900s was a pretty raw coal mining town. The little sandy main street had a church at one end, with the underground coal mine's 'Poppet Head' structure rising up into the sky nearby, and, at the other extremity (in all senses of that word), another place of congregation – the pub. Dotted around the area were rough mining cottages – two-bedroom affairs, tin roof and timber walls – and a scattering of Maori whares. Mining was the predominant occupation, with the brickworks (producing the famous 'Huntly Brick') becoming an important employer around 1909.

School was immediately alongside the main trunk railway line, and twice the wooden Huntly Primary School was burned down by sparks from wood- and coal-fired steam trains that huffed and chuffed though the centre of town.

May Shaw (née Ranby, formerly of Ohaupo) was a young single woman who taught primary school at Huntly in a large enclosed tent. The single temporary 'classroom' and facilities were very rudimentary and the 120 (generally unwilling) pupils were of mixed ages and nationalities, many of them local Maori children. This teaching scenario was quite a challenge for a young lass. However, although May was physically diminutive, she was not lacking in strength of character and on a normal teaching day she was well able to cope with its rigours.

One of May's many challenges was the cultural differences between the various nationalities. For Maori kids superstition was a normal part of life; a piwakawaka (fantail) or ruru (morepork) coming into the whare or home was regarded as signalling either pending bad luck or an imminent death – depending on what you wanted to believe. Of even more significance, was the taipo – expressed locally in the term 'mangumangu taipo' – or the devil, and the parental threat of this would have young Maori kids rolling their eyes in fear.

On one not-so-normal day, while May was teaching, a steam train stopped at the adjacent Huntly Rail Station and for some reason it happened to have an elephant on board. It could have been with a circus – May never did find out – but certainly seeing an elephant in New Zealand in that era would have been a very rare event, if not a unique sight.

Trains, on the other hand, were commonplace, and the sounds of the chuffing and panting of the steam engine from beside the closed walls of the tent evoked little interest. However, as the train sat idling in the station, the elephant raised its trunk back over its head and let out a *massive* blast of sound – 'OOOOOOOOOO OOOWHEEEEEEEEEEEEEEEEEEWWWWWWWW' – and a wave of kids bolted out the back of the tent as if the hounds of hell were after them. The stampede was led by the Maori kids but the Pakeha kids unthinkingly joined the exodus.

A bewildered May tried to stop them, but as far as the Maori kids were concerned the oft-threatened mangumangu taipo had finally appeared, and in spades. The stampede headed for home, or the hills, and within seconds the bewildered teacher was completely alone.

It was days and days before she had a full class again. Wall-eyed and spooked children gradually re-appeared: crept, coerced or dragged back to that tent from whence the devil had appeared. And the sound of a steam train arriving at the Huntly station evoked class nervousness for months after the 'elephant train' had disappeared.

The Old Lynch Homestead, Huntly.

76

39 The LIST

*You probably have a story of your own about the physiological torture the god-botherers practice. They turn up on the first Sunday of **every** month and have this uncanny ability to arrive at your door at the worst possible time – and their practice of walking up the drive, children attached and clasping the latest brochure 'Our Way', or whatever, can be unnerving and often very inopportune. Which is why people get really pissed off with them.*

This particular event happened mid-summer when it was as hot as hell and typically Waikato-muggy. You're sitting in your undergruds on the sofa, unshaven, beer in hand, watching the live motor racing. You hear a knock at the door. With startling clarity you realise a) you're about naked; b) there're two women and two innocent-looking young girls staring at you through the open French doors and c) there's nowhere to go. And, bugger it all, they're the god-botherers – again! Course it doesn't help that you know they're still on a high cos they've just come from Ruth's place and she's had them in for a cuppa and a friendly theological debate. So the combination of shame, frustration and the fact that your

'time out' has been trashed means they're gonna get a serve … big time – iff'n there's no hole in your jocks.

Or, there's the time you came in for lunch and somehow mum and you end up in the front room having an impromptu look for that grubscrew by the spare bed. The first you know there's been a visitor is when mum finds 'Our Way' hastily dropped by the sliding glass doors. Ooh no, it's not the first Sunday of the month again is it?

——— *** ———

Andy and his dad, Stephen, out on the farm at Karapiro had requested to be placed on the 'blacklist' of properties *not* to be visited. (You probably didn't know there is such a list did you? Well the phone number is … nah, you like the visits every first Sunday don't ya?). Both of them had repeatedly requested to NOT be visited at all. Never. Ever.

Despite this, one spring Andy's down the middle of the farm trying to draft out a calving heifer that's determined to stay with the mob. He sees a strange car parked on the race leading up to the house and, having thrown his drafting stick four paddocks away in frustration, heads up to see who the hell is visiting in the middle of a dirty, wet spring. And stuff me it's the god-botherers! Suit and bloody tie would you believe. And the blind fool wants to debate theology – ignoring the Honda's ice breaker-like bow wave of slush and Andy's body language clearly saying this is not a good time to be here.

To give the man his due, he did eventually realise that he was not welcome and he beat a retreat back to the car. While helping the well-intentioned 'botherer' back to his car, Andy 'inadvertently' boosts the advocate flat out into the slurry of mud 'n shit on the side of the cow race.

That evening when the BIG god-botherer Bossman rings to remonstrate with him about the unprovable assistance Andy lays the law down about NO VISITS and a permanent non-molestation promise is reached.

However, a few months later Andy's dad Stephen, up at the other farm house, had his Sunday afternoon nap interrupted by yet another foursome of fanatics. Being a former Desert Rat with Monty had instilled a very assertive personality in Stephen and this 'take no prisoners' attitude would remain with him for life. A succinct eviction message was issued along with a stern directive not to go up to the other (Andy's) house – something the foursome promptly ignored.

So, when the local policeman finally arrives at the scene he finds a perfect imprint of a knobbly chestnut walking stick cratered right across the roof of the evangelist's car. Deeply. Very deeply. To the point that the roof was beyond repair and a $1,000 roof transplant was required from another vehicle.

So how did Stephen extract himself from a GBH (grievous 'car'-body harm) charge? Well, those war wounds sure can play up unexpectedly. He hobbles out to the cop with his stick supporting his obviously semi-invalided body and reminiscences at some length about the sacrifices he made for God and country. Stephen then explains that in his anger and haste to evict the interlopers he had leapt off his ATV motorbike, tripped and in reaching out to save himself, inadvertently laid his cane ('me war wounds ya know') across the car's roof. Riiiight!

They finally made THE LIST.

And what of all us others who haven't made the black list? Well, mum's learnt to close the curtains at lunchtime, the dogs go beserk at the words 'Our Way' and many rural people subconsciously spend Sundays looking over their shoulders. And me – well, I couldn't get up off the couch 'cause I wasn't sure whether I had that pair of holey undies on. So in a moment of weakness I agreed to look at their magazine.

And what do I do on Sundays now? 'Here brother, while I'm talking to you, let me show you the latest copy of "Our Way".'

40 **The Champg**

Blackie milked cows in a walkthrough cowshed right up to the early '80s. By the time a man has punched cows for nearly fifty years you'd think he'd have seen 'em all.

Well, that was before Aimee's Frisky Delight, or number 78 for short. Frisky was an understatement. She was (and I *am* talking in the past tense) just a copper-plated bitch. Somehow, pet calf-club calves either grow up to be lousy producers or mean-spirited, or both. This one had been Grand Champion at the A & P Show and so had a pedigree to match the Royal family. A real show stopper in more ways than one.

As a newly calved heifer in the milking herd Frisky was nasty, bless her departed soul. She kicked and kicked. Leg ropes, belly ropes, tail locks, even Blackie doing a touch of ear biting in a moment of extreme provocation. Don't know whether he ever resorted to a Hopuati league-tackle but he sure as hell tried everything else.

One day the neighbour

happened along in the midst of the daily rodeo. His sage advice was to give her a sharp smack between the ears with something good and solid.

'End of problem every time – guaranteed! But not too hard, mind.'

The rationale behind this is that a moment or two of unconsciousness is useful time out for the offender to reflect on her evil ways.

So, a few days later the same neighbour calls into the cowshed at the end of milking. Blackie rushes out to greet him and after a while it dawns on the advice-giver that Blackie is sort of fluttering around in front of him. The neighbour kicks the ground, damns the weather and sort of moves around a bit more. Blackie mirror-images him. Finally, sensing

something untoward, the neighbour peers over Blackie's shoulder and … Frisky is upside-down in the bale – likely dead. Ah, there's a tow rope on one leg and the Fergies lined up outside the yard.

Embarrassed at being the instigator, the neighbour pretends he hasn't seen the cadaver and clears out for an urgent appointment.

I guess that's one milking that was easy to put the cups on – Frisky all laid out like she's sunbathing on her back.

Blackie often recalls the good days of milking in a walk-through cowshed.

Aimee's Frisky Delight? You know that A & P Grand Champion you bred? Must have earned you a fortune with her breeding?

'Oh yer, I think she drowned in the creek or sumfing. Damned shame – best heifer I ever had.'